Giovanni Archeaggi

SANGUINE AFFAIR

Giovanni Andreazzi

authorHOUSE®

AuthorHouse™
1663 Liberty Drive, Suite 200
Bloomington, IN 47403
www.authorhouse.com
Phone: 1-800-839-8640

First published by AuthorHouse   7/15/2008

ISBN: 978-1-4343-6617-7 (sc)
ISBN: 978-1-4343-6618-4 (hc)

Printed in the United States of America
Bloomington, Indiana

This book is printed on acid-free paper.

TXu 1-571-923

DEDICATION

This book is for all of our AHS class of '62 classmates who are no longer in our company. They are in my thoughts and prayers, and I hope that they enjoyed their lives as much as I am enjoying mine now.

ACKNOWLEDGEMENTS

The hardest job in getting a book produced is the editing. An editor must be able to read words that he or she may not have any interest in and do it with an open mind. I can read my own manuscript several times and still not catch all the errors. Of course an editor cannot catch all the errors either, but they will see the document with fresh eyes. Having someone who also can provide comments as to whether the book makes sense is also desirable. My editor, Roberta, who also worked with me on *Fairy Tales and Sea Stories,* was able to do just that. So, I hope she will continue to be my editor as long as I am able to write my stories. Thank you, Roberta.

Thanks go also to Kris at the local Dunkin' Donuts for her encouragement and nice words. This is the first time I have given a manuscript to someone other than my editor for comments. Although she was kind enough to say that she liked it, she may have been just being nice to a regular customer.

Finally, a big thank you goes to Ginny Abblett, who, years ago, lived a couple of blocks from where I grew up and was always afraid of the strange boy in the Watson Woods (yours truly). She is the artist who did the front and back covers, capturing the title of the book as I had pictured it while being far too kind with the image on the back cover. She is a much better artist than I am a writer and has lots of other drawings for sale at her website:

http://ginnyabblett.com/

INTRODUCTION

BLOODY. THAT'S WHAT I think "sanguine" means, although dictionaries give the first meaning as "the color of blood; red." "Cheerfully confident or optimistic" is usually the second listed. "Affair" can mean "something done or to be done; business," or, "a romantic and sexual relationship by two people not married." So the title of this book can potentially have at least four meanings, depending on the reader's interpretation: a bloody business, a bloody romantic relationship, a cheerful affair or, a cheerful business. Any one, I suppose, will do.

This book is a sequel to my first novel, *Dedra,* continuing a short time after that story stopped. The reader who finished *Dedra* thinking that the two main characters lived happily ever after may be surprised with the beginning of *Sanguine Affair.*

If you purchased this book, I sincerely thank you. Rest assured that I have not yet made a bundle from any of my other four books, as my per-book royalties are less than two dollars. If I do make any money, the IRS will get their hands on some of it, but most will be given away so what the government takes will be a lot less. I have enough money for my needs, and, as Andrew Carnegie said, "The man who dies rich, dies disgraced."

The story herein is just words, words connected together to form a picture created from my own imagination, or more likely, a compilation of experiences, stored by my subconscious throughout my life. Stored away, but not forgotten. Now, when I have more time to think rather than react, my mind is regurgitating this store of thoughts in a random order so that I somehow am able to put thoughts together, like a connect-the-dots picture, into the semblance of a story. Although I lapse in and out of the first person (my English teachers would cringe at that), I do so for a reason. The story is not real, nor is it about me. You should not be afraid of my imagination, unless you too, can imagine.

CHAPTER ONE

WHEN THEY FOUND THE body, there was a message next to it decorated with the victim's blood.

"What the hell do ya think that means?" Deputy Dag asked. He was named in memory of his great uncle, Dag Hammarskjöld, who, in the 1950's, was the Secretary-General of the United Nations. Great Uncle Dag was killed in 1961 when his plane crashed near the border between Katanga and North Rhodesia.

It was a shame he didn't inherit his uncle's intelligence or reasoning skills. The lack of good genes from that side of the family had, the last ten years, kept him from advancing beyond deputy in the small Ohio farm town of Devola, outside of Marietta, near the Ohio River and across from West Virginia.

Dag was a pale-skinned, pot-bellied man in his early forties. He had a bulbous nose reminiscent of W. C. Fields and ears with large lobes that hung down like those on his hunting dog. He spoke with a slight West Virginia accent which he probably had picked up playing with his cousins on the other side of the river. He was more comfortable taking a nap in his chair at the station than pursuing criminals, but came alive when fishing for catfish on the northern banks of the Ohio River.

What they were looking at was a piece of paper with drops of the victims blood drizzled along the outside border. It formed a bizarre sort of crimson gild around the writing in the middle. The numbers were neatly printed on an eight-and-a-half-by-eleven sheet of plain white printer paper, common to most office supply stores.

16	16	31	16	16
31	4	4	31	0
31	20	20	31	0
16	16	31	16	16
31	21	21	14	0
31	0	0	0	0
16	16	31	16	16
31	17	17	17	0
31	4	4	31	0
31	17	17	14	0
31	21	21	17	0
29	21	21	23	0
31	21	21	17	0
16	8	4	8	16
31	21	21	17	0
31	17	17	14	0
31	0	0	0	0
16	16	31	16	16

"I don't know what that means," replied Sheriff Vince VanGofer. "Your guess is as good as mine. Has the coroner been notified?"

Vince was a good looking, dark skinned, lean man. He was about the same age as Deputy Dag, but much more intelligent and ambitious. He had numerous relatives and friends in and around Devola which was how he got elected as Washington County Sheriff. He, too, liked to catfish, but that was a common pastime along the Ohio River.

"Yep," the deputy said. Dag was smart enough to follow procedures, which included stringing crime scene tape around the area and not touching anything after verifying the victim was dead. Determining that she was dead was the easiest part since her heart, or an object resembling a human heart, presumably from the victim, was lying next to her body. There was also a gaping hole in her chest where, again, presumably, the heart had resided before being dislodged.

When he first arrived on the scene by himself, Dag was glad he had made it well away from the area he later taped, twenty fast paces to where he "spilled his cookies" right after he saw the victim. It was actually cookies he blew out on the ground having had several peanut butter patties his wife had bought from the neighbor's daughter who was a Girl Scout. He had never seen someone so brutally cut open before and hoped to God he never would again. He was sure some critter would clean up the spilled cookies later that night. Raccoons and possums were not picky eaters, which he had witnessed after they raided his garbage can a few times.

"We're going to have to get the experts from Columbus down here to investigate," Sheriff Vince said. The town of Marietta, population 14,000, was the seat of Washington County, population just over sixty thousand. The town did not have a large, crime-scene investigation team nor much need for one. There was precious little industry in the town, which was the last Ohio exit on I-77 before crossing the bridge into West Virginia. It would be at least three hours before a team, 125 miles away, got organized and made their way southeast to Marietta.

While Sheriff Vince stepped away to use his cell phone to call Columbus, the deputy moved into the crime-scene area. He stepped over the body, being careful not to disturb anything. He bent down and stared at the victim's still open eyes, now clouded over like those of a three-day-old fish. The tears which had kept them clear during life, had dried into

3

a milky haze. The victim's mouth was as open as the eyes displaying a well-maintained set of teeth, bright white from many trips to the dentist. He didn't understand America's fixation on having the whitest smile money could buy. To him, that seemed a waste of effort since all his older relatives had lost their teeth after the age of sixty. A clean set of teeth was one thing, but abnormally white was not for him. *She can take those pearly whites to the pearly gates with her now*, he thought, then snickered at the thought.

Sheriff Vince returned after using the cell phone. He had gone almost all the way to the patrol car as though he wanted to avoid disturbing the victim's resting place, but actually he just walked to where the signal was strong enough to connect to a cell tower.

"Columbus has someone on the way," he related to Dag. "It seems they have an investigator needing some experience who is available now."

The two continued talking and gesturing as he watched them from the hill almost two miles away. He could make out some of their conversation because of his ability to read lips, a skill he had picked up since his hearing had started to go bad after taking antibiotics for an infection he had acquired at the Padre Island Sea Shore in Texas.

He had received some nasty jellyfish stings while wading from the shore right after Dee, the love of his life, and her daughter had gone down on Flight 800. The ill-fated flight had hit the water off the coast of Long Island shortly after taking off from JFK. The official cause of the crash remained unknown, but witnesses testified they had seen a bright streak in the sky before the jet exploded into a ball of flame. Through some sloppy listing on the airline's part, Dee and her daughter had been listed as "unknown passengers" and that is the way he wanted it to stay.

Dee had called him from her cell phone to let him know

they had gotten the last two standby seats and they were both in first class. She was excited to be going to France to do a little sightseeing and a lot of shopping with Dedra. He had been to France before and didn't care for the place. He had seen all the sights, eaten all the food (the only food he would want again were the Grand Marnier-flavored, chocolate-filled crepes from the sidewalk vendors), and he hated to shop, so Dee and Dedra were on their own. Dee actually didn't mind, and after their whirlwind romance during which they had stuck to each other like conjoined twins, she welcomed the opportunity to separate for a short time. The trip without him also offered her some quality time with Dedra.

He, too, welcomed the break from the routine of seeing Dee every day, all day long. So, a year after they re-united (Dee was not aware they had met before), Dee and Dedra had boarded a flight that had gone into the cold Atlantic a mere eleven minutes after it had taken off. Like so many others who had perished that day, their bodies were never found. All were claimed by the sea.

The loss of Dee turned him sour, even more than the first time. The first time he had met Dee, he had already killed many women, among them, Dee's daughter, Dedra. He had been able to find a way to erase all the evil he had done giving him and all his victims, including Dedra, a second chance at life. This time, he wasn't going to look for a way out from the evil he had done anew, and that which he was about to do. He did want to have fun before someone figured out what the numbers he provided with each of his victims meant, and then discovered who he was and tracked him down.

Until then, he was going to "get even" with all the girls he blamed for his inadequacies, all those girls in his high school class who had ignored him, all those girls who had never given him a second look because he had no money, all those girls who had ignored him because he wasn't cool, had no car, and wore essentially the same clothes day after day. Kate was the first to go and he had to admit her heart was tender after all these years. He was able to bite through it without much effort even though it was slippery with blood and was still trying to pump blood through empty arteries.

The deputy and the sheriff didn't think to scan the hills around the murder scene. Even if they had, he would be difficult to see nestled in the trees some distance away. The trees were bare of leaves allowing him a nearly unobstructed view of the area. In his camouflaged hunting suit, he would be nearly invisible from where the two were hunched over her body. Winter was almost over in southern Ohio. Buds were already forming on the maple trees and soon the white blossoms of the apple trees, growing wild in the woods, would blanket the area.

He would lie there until sunset, about an hour, and then walk away as carefully as possible not attracting any attention. He had his hearing aids in so he could hear nearly as well as anyone else who happened to be walking around, especially hunters. There wouldn't be too many of them this close to dusk and so far away from any hunting season. He only had to go down the hill and follow the Muskingum River to his car near Route 60. Then it was a short drive on back roads to I-77 and off to his next destination. He would have liked to stay around for the action, but he had places to go and more girls to meet. His next stop would be Raleigh, North Carolina.

When she arrived, Investigator Ginny (short for Virginia) Joynt, got out of her car and scanned the hills surrounding the area. Had he been using ordinary binoculars without the anti-reflective coating, she might have seen the sun reflecting off the glass, but she noticed nothing. Deputy Dag met her and introduced himself.

"I'm Deputy Dag," he said, unsure whether to extend his hand for a shake or not. He was not expecting a woman and his limited experience in law enforcement did not include working with a woman as an equal, or maybe in this case a superior. She was from a different jurisdiction and outranked him in grade.

She was rail thin, tall, and quite attractive. Her almond shaped face was framed by long brown hair parted in the middle. Her nose was out of proportion to her other petite features, but none the less complimented her large brown eyes and full lips.

"Hi," she said. "I'm Investigator Ginny Joynt." She had noticed his uneasiness and extended her own hand which he shook, a little too hard. "Where is the body?"

"This way," he said. He let go of her hand, but not before he started to turn, throwing her off balance. She didn't fall, but stumbled trying to take a step in his direction. She was relieved to be at a crime scene where there were no reporters, their cameras looking at her every move and catching her nearly falling. This was only her fifth murder investigation and the first on her own, so she was a little nervous.

"Would you help me with my equipment?" she asked. "It's in the trunk."

"Sure," he said, and wheeled back around. She opened the trunk of the car and handed him the camera, a new digital one the department had purchased with some drug money that had become property of the county after a dealer was put safely behind bars. She grabbed the tool box, which was a lot heavier than the camera, but not too much for her to handle.

"That it?" the deputy asked.

"Yep," she said, and slammed the trunk lid. Deputy Dag led the way up the small incline to where the body lay.

"I already took some pictures," he said. "I can take more with your camera."

"If you don't mind," she said, grateful for the help. "I need some to take back with me."

She was again thankful there were no reporters to record her getting sick as soon as she saw the partly eaten heart and open chest of the woman lying on the ground. She puked only a few feet from the same place Deputy Dag had done just four hours or so earlier. Her protein spill was just that, a Big Mac she had consumed after stopping at a McDonalds on her way out of Columbus. With the Big Mac, she spilled nearly all the coffee she had had since she had gotten up that morning.

She normally didn't eat fast food, but had skipped breakfast, and after this, would most likely miss dinner. A Big Mac had just sounded good and was something she hadn't had in a long time. After leaving it in the woods just a few feet away, she probably wouldn't have another for a long time to come. She felt embarrassed about getting sick at the sight of the woman's body, but she had never seen anything that gruesome on her other cases. Had the deputy confided in her that he had had the same reaction, she might have felt a little less inferior, but his male superiority complex had kept him from uttering a word. She couldn't wait to show the crime scene photographs to her counterparts back in Columbus and watch their reactions.

While she was composing herself, the Deputy used her camera to take several pictures and then handed the camera to her. She took a few more from different angles just to be sure she had enough. Pictures wouldn't solve the case but were excellent memory joggers should this case ever get to a courtroom.

"That's interesting," she said, pointing an un-adorned, long index finger at the paper with the numbers on it.

"Any idea what it means?" Vince asked.

"It's obviously a code of some kind," she responded. "But it's not intuitively obvious to me what it's about." She set her camera down and opened the box she had carried with her from the car. She slid open one of the drawers taking out some long forceps and then opened the top compartment and took out a large plastic bag. Using the forceps, she carefully picked up the paper and slid it into the bag and zipped it up.

"Where's the coroner?" she asked. Usually the ambulance and coroner were on the scene by the time she arrived, but she and these two cops were the only ones here.

"He's on his way now," Vince said. "There was a bad accident on the highway and someone was killed. All the available ambulances were there too since a couple of other people were injured. We told him this was not urgent since this girl's not goin' nowhere. He said he would let us know when he was on the way and called not two minutes before you showed up."

As if on cue, they turned to see the ambulance coming toward them followed by a man on a motorcycle.

"That would be him now," the deputy said. "His butt's practically stuck to that Harley."

She put the plastic encased paper into a drawer in the box and took out a pair of surgical gloves. Putting them on, she bent to the task of examining the woman's body. She fought back gags as she picked up the heart and put it in a bag.

"You think some critter did that?" the deputy asked.

"Don't know for sure," she responded. "But it looks more like human teeth marks to me." She only had the memory of pictures she had seen to help make that assumption. They were of another woman's breast that the nipple had been bitten off by a rapist before he had killed the prostitute. "An animal most likely would have carried the heart off to eat somewhere else." She set the heart aside so that the coroner could remove it with the body.

When she said "human," the two men just looked at each other.

Next, she felt under and around the woman for any clues. The fact that the victim was completely naked helped because there were no clothes to search. She found nothing and finished her inspection as the coroner arrived with the ambulance crew and a stretcher.

"That the victims heart?" the coroner asked.

"We can only assume at this point," she said.

"This is Investigator Joynt, from Columbus," Vince said, talking to the coroner.

"Glad to make your acquaintance," the coroner said, without giving her his name. He wore thick glasses which rested halfway down a large nose. His mustache added to the features making him look like Mr. Whipple from the toilet paper advertisements.

"I guess I can pronounce her dead without even examining her vital signs," the coroner said, "but I'd better go through the motions anyway."

"I'm through with my exam," Ginny said standing up and taking off her gloves.

The last rays of the setting sun were filtering through the trees as the uniformed ambulance attendants placed the body and heart into a rubberized bag and took it away.

CHAPTER TWO

THE DAY STARTED MUCH as the other four hundred seventy two had, more than a year and four months, since I had lost the only woman I had ever loved in a tragic plane crash off the coast of Long Island. I turned off the reading light that I had left on when I had drifted off to sleep the night before. I removed the finished book from my chest, and dragged myself out of bed, slowly at first. I then mustered enough momentum to stand and make it to the bathroom. I looked in the mirror.

When will you stop mourning? I thought to myself. *You have to put your miserable life back together soon, before it's too late.*

My employer, Macon Engineering, was good enough to give me 'as much time as you need,' my boss had said, 'to get yourself back together.' I don't think he meant more than a year. It was just a matter of time before someone from personnel would call and tell me to pick up my personal effects in a box. A box the guard would have in his shack at the entrance to the complex. It didn't matter. I had gone back to work after winning the lottery only to keep busy and to have human contact. I didn't want much human contact now, nor did staying busy matter much any more.

This morning I was at least able to brush my teeth, comb my hair, and push an electric shaver (badly in need of new blades) across my beard. Today I was able to restrain the tears that came so easily these many months. I was "presentable" now, presentable enough to leave the apartment and do a couple of the only "sane" activities I continued doing after Dee's death. Activities we used to do together, but now I did them alone, alone in my own sadness and grief.

I was lucky enough, if lucky is the word, to have won enough money in the lottery such that I didn't have to work. It was a lot of money paid out over twenty years, which I could have taken in a lump sum, but wanted to leave a respectable income for Dee, my wife, if something happened to me. If something happened to both of us then her only heir, Dedra, from Dee's first marriage, her "starter husband" as Dee would say it, would inherit the remainder. I had no children, and therefore no heirs of my own. I hadn't planned on out-living my wife, but life does throw some nasty curves at you from time to time. Sadly, Dedra had been on the same flight as her mother.

My check, mailed to me from Macon Engineering, paid for food, rent, and utilities for the furnished apartment I was living in with enough left over for gasoline when I drove to the beach, and, of course, dog food. I couldn't stay in the condo Dee and I had lived in, a condo I couldn't bear to visit but once a month or so because of all the good memories. All of the bills for the condo, including the association fees which took care of the yard, were automatically deducted from the bank account where the winnings were being deposited. I imagined the winnings were probably amounting to a small fortune by now. Before the accident the winnings were "fun" money like for Dee's and her daughter's trip to France for sightseeing and shopping. We gave a lot of money away anonymously to various charities because we didn't want to become rich, spoiled, or famous.

Dog food, you ask? Yes, dog food. The supermarket clerks must have thought I owned the biggest dog in the world, or several big dogs. I bought eighty pounds of dog food a week, two large bags. This came to eleven pounds of dog food a day, and I did not have one dog. I had started buying the dog food the week after Flight 800 went down.

Dee could have purchased their two first-class seats in advance, but the trip was a spur-of-the-moment one. Dee was famous for her impulsive behavior and the trip to Paris was no exception. So she had grabbed her daughter, gone to the airport, found a flight that evening, and purchased two standby fares in first class with cash. There had been two cancellations, so she and Dedra were allowed to board. They took only their hand-carry bags with a few necessities and planned on buying anything else they needed in Paris. Dedra's French was passable and with an almost unlimited bank account Dee could throw enough money around to find a five-star hotel which 'just happened to have a room.'

To start day four hundred-seventy three, I put on a light jacket, left my one-bedroom second-floor apartment, and walked across the street to the Barnes and Noble bookstore. Even though I lived in Corpus Christi, Texas, it usually was cold enough on the first of November to require some protection from the weather. I would spend the better part of the morning at B&N, drinking my favorite comfort beverage and perusing the books. I would search until I found a promising book, one that would keep me entertained, which usually meant occupying my mind until I fell asleep with the book on my chest and the reading light on.

"The usual?" the clerk behind the counter asked. The usual meant a decaf, white-chocolate, soy, mocha, venti, fixed by the dark-haired, PYT (purdy-young-thang) in a B&N green apron. I could not drink real milk anymore because of my "condition," which was diagnosed as "lactose intolerance," a polite way of saying I had green-apple quickstep after drinking the real thing. I drank only decaf, because I had become sensitive to caffeine after overdosing on it standing mid-watches during my short time in the Navy.

"Yes-please-thank-you," I responded, almost saying it as one four-syllable word. *My God,* I thought, *I've been doing the same thing so often, she knows what I want. They don't know who I am, but what I am, the-guy-who-drinks-the-same-thing-every-morning-at-the-same-time person.* Like a robot, I placed a five-dollar bill on the counter. I proceeded to the "Pick Up Here" sign hanging from a chain attached to the tee-bars in the acoustical ceiling grid. The PYT knew I always left her the change from the $3.29-including-tax drink. For the generous tip, I usually got an extra squirt from the white-chocolate syrup bottle.

I pretended to drool over the many pastries and chocolates under glass while the PYT frothed my soy. I would like to consume one each of the pastries, but the venti was the only vice I allowed myself and at seven-hundred calories, it was enough. I had the hunger, but since Dee's death, like the desire for making love, the desire to eat sweets was gone. Beside that, even in my grief I was weight conscious. In fact, I had lost at least ten pounds since the mock funeral I had conducted myself, tossing a bouquet of chrysanthemums, Dee's favorite, into the water near Westhampton Beach on Long Island. Like the other eighty-eight passengers, Dee's and Dedra's bodies had not been found. Funeral services for the "knowns" were held at the side of a boat in the harbor where the plane had gone down. They 'sleep with the fishes,' was what Clemenza said of Luca Brasi in *The Godfather*. Tears started to well up as I reached for the proffered venti the PYT placed on the shoulder-high counter.

"Are you all right?" the PYT asked. Even she noticed the tears forming in my eyes. After several months of coming to

B&N, I still did not know the PYT's name. Worse yet, I didn't care. Not wanting her to hear the quaver in my voice, exposing the fact that I was not all right, I hesitated while I slipped an insulating corrugated collar around the paper cup. After another second, I swallowed the hard lump in my throat.

"I'm fine," I responded, not offering an explanation. I took my venti and headed for the shelves of books in the non-fiction section. I usually read only fiction. That venue offered an escape from the harsh reality of the last nine months. But this time, I decided to see if something that wasn't a fabrication would pique my interest. Holding my venti in my left hand, I cocked my head slightly toward my right shoulder, making the titles easier to read. I touched the spines of the books with my free right hand, as if that would make the words come alive.

I was about to give up on non-fiction and head for the other shelves, which promised an escape from reality, when a small book caught my eye. I should say it caught my index finger first, for it truly was a small book. The book was so thin, there was no title on the edge. The color was a blood red and as I looked a little closer, I saw the skeleton of a finger on the spine.

I recognized the second metacarpal, proximal phalanx, middle phalanx, and distal bones that make up the index finger. I knew the bones well, having broken both phalanx bones in a sailing boat accident in 1996. I had wrapped a one-inch line around my hand and fingers to get a better grip when the ship's skipper had, during a docking maneuver, reversed the engine. My refusal to let go cost me the use of my right hand for six weeks, a lesson I would never forget. I took a sip of my venti while I worked my healed index finger and thumb around the little hard-backed book. I pulled it out and read the title.

"*El Dia De Los Muertos,*" I read aloud. *Day of the dead,* I translated the Spanish in my head. I had had three years of Spanish in high school, twenty-five years ago, but had forgotten most of what I had learned. I still did retain just enough to make my translations passable, but shoddy to say the least. I was reasonably sure this did mean "day of the dead."

I took the little book to a table in the back of the coffee shop. The PYT smiled at me when I returned, passing by the 'Order Here' sign. I sat down, took a sip of my venti, set the cup down, and opened the little book. Thankfully, the inside was not in Spanish. In the third year of high school Spanish class, the class had read a book titled *El Sombrero De Tres Picos*, which translated to *The Hat With Three Points*. I did not remember what it was about and certainly could not translate an entire book again.

I reached the bottom of my second venti at the same time I finished the book. *El Dia* was a story of a man's trip to a beach during the Mexican holiday honoring the dead, October thirty-first through November second. At some time during those three days, he met the spirits of his dead relatives returning to celebrate with him. The story was told in the third person, for the man was never seen again. A note was found on the beach telling of his encounters, with a warning, *tenga el cuidado en el dia de los muertos*, at the bottom of the note. He did not leave an explanation of what the reader was to "take care with" on the day of the dead.

My venti gone, I put the book back and left the bookstore and the PYT. I was now ready to do the second sane thing that kept me on the shallow end of the pool. I entered my apartment just long enough to use the bathroom and pick up some dog food. I could have relieved myself in the bookstore restroom, but it was usually dirty. I did not enjoy using the facilities where my feet "stuck" to the floor. I did not think standing in someone else's excrement and then tracking it into your own living space was a healthy thing to do. I had left without a book to read myself to sleep with tonight, but I had a spare on my nightstand, kept for those days I came home from B&N empty handed.

When I opened the pantry door to get the dog food,

I saw that the current bag was nearly empty. I had two other forty-pound bags, but the remaining contents of the open bag would suffice. I picked up the near-empty bag and left the apartment, still wearing the jacket I had donned before going to B&N. With a push of the button on the remote car-door alarm key holder, the lights on my Humvee flashed twice and the horn sounded the same number of times. Admittedly, a Hummer was a bit of overkill for driving on the beach at Padre Island, but a four-wheeler was required to go as far away from the occupied area as I wanted to go.

By the time I was over the bridge on South Padre Island Drive, it was already one o'clock. I didn't plan on eating anything until I returned around six that night. It would already be getting dark by then, and I might have an appetite. Long gone were the days when I could eat several bagel sandwiches at a time. I continued south on the paved portion of the road, passing all the condos to the right. The condos stopped at the point where the National Seashore began. As I ran out of paved road, I came upon the sign indicating "Four-Wheel Drive Vehicles Only, Beyond This Point."

I drove a short distance more. There was no one else in sight. I could see almost as far as Corpus to the north and Mexico to the south. As soon as I pulled to a stop, the seagulls started to gather. It reminded me of Alfred Hitchcock's movie, *The Birds*. They recognized the Hummer and knew I was there to feed them. Within minutes there were hundreds of squawking birds surrounding me as I stepped from the Hummer. They knew the routine, one I called "tunneling." I would walk into the wind carrying a pail of dog food, this time a bag, and feed the gulls. Today the wind was out of the north, so I walked towards Corpus dropping pellets as I went. In seconds, I was walking in a tunnel of seagulls. They were flying alongside me, above me, behind me, and some even in front. They couldn't resist the high protein food I brought them, even at the risk of touching a human's hand. At less than fifty cents a pound, it was a cheap way to get this commingling-with-nature sensation.

In addition to dropping the dog food, I held out my hand filled with pellets, first right, then left. The gulls would dip and take the food right from my hand. Their beaks were hard and they were not gentle creatures. More than once they unintentionally formed welts with their ravenous pecks but rarely had drawn blood. Tossing some of the pellets in the air behind me brought more squawks than merely dropping the pellets. It was noisier than teen-aged girls at a Beatles concert. The gulls flew so close their wings touched the top of my head and my outstretched arms. Tunneling was an incredible experience, one that made me forget how miserable I had felt since Dee's departure from life. My earth-bound flight with the gulls was about to end since I was near the bottom of the bag. I had walked almost a mile, trailing birds as I went. As I was reaching for the last handful of pellets, the gulls suddenly left as quickly as they had appeared. This usually happened when someone was walking a dog and they got too close, but there was no one else and no dog.

I was now alone on the beach. I turned the bag up and dumped the remaining pellets on the sand thinking that would bring them back, but no gulls appeared. *That's strange,* I thought. *Nothing like this has happened before. Something has scared them.* I turned and headed back toward the Hummer.

Then, just as suddenly as the seagulls' disappearance, the wind became dead calm. I noticed too, that there were no sandpipers darting back and forth with the waves trying to catch the mussels before they dug their way to safety in the wet sand. But there would be no need now for the little birds to dart. There were no waves. The gulf was completely calm. It was like a mirror reflecting the hazy humidity of the evaporating water. *I've never seen the gulf this calm. At ebb tide there aren't as many waves, but it still has swells and moves in and out. I don't like this one bit. Wait a minute! What day is this?* I checked my Rolex look-alike watch, the one Dee had given me for Christmas last year. The date window indicated November second. *This is the third and last day of the day of the dead.*

This is stupid, I thought. *It's just a pagan Aztec ritual infused with the Catholic Church's All Souls Day,* I remembered from the book. The Aztecs had kept their own beliefs, but to please the Spaniards, adopted the Christian holidays which were celebrated by the Catholics in Mexico.

My thoughts were interrupted by the unpredictable gulf. Waves were again approaching the shore now. Only this time they were not the pleasant looking waves that had preceded the calm. They were the greenish-gray looking waves indicative of a storm far out at sea, a storm or a hurricane. *But there was no hurricane or I would have seen it last night on the news.* As the first waves crashed ashore I noticed the gulf in the distance was calm again. Then the wind picked up, not as strong as before, and changed directions coming easterly from off the gulf. I tilted my head as I thought I heard something above the noise of the wind. I did hear something, a voice carried on the wind. A voice, but what was it saying?

"B-e-w-a-r-e," whispered the wind. "B-e-w-a-r-e t-h-e d-a-y o-f t-h-e d-e-a-d." Chills ran up my spine, and goose bumps rose on my arms. "B-e-w-a-r-e t-h-e d-a-y o-f t-h-e d-e-a-d."

By now, I was almost a half mile from the Hummer. *Returning to the Hummer will get me away from this craziness.* I thought. I was looking down at the sand when the last of the waves crashed ashore. *Maybe there was a submarine out there doing that, passing too fast and too close to shore under the water, or maybe a whale. A sub could be in the gulf, but not a whale. It's too warm a body of water for whales.* My mind was racing now.

"B-e-w-a-r-e t-h-e d-a-y o-f t-h-e d-e-a-d."

I don't scare easily, but the strange circumstances I found myself surrounded by this second day in November were unsettling. The gulf was again like glass, not a creature was in sight. The warnings were being carried by the wind. I was now heading for the Hummer at a trot. As I was nearing the Hummer and safety, ripples appeared out in the water to my left, thousands of individual ripples, as if fish were swimming very close to the surface. *Fish*, I thought. *At least there is something else out here, besides me.*

But it wasn't fish.

"B-e-w-a-r-e t-h-e d-a-y o-f t-h-e d-e-a-d."

Soon heads replaced the ripples. Thousands of heads, followed by shoulders, then chests, then arms, until entire bodies appeared. Behind them were more heads, and behind them more ripples. There were men, women, and children, all dressed differently. There were conquistadors in armor, there were sailors, there were women in frontier dresses, there were men and women in business suits, and there were others. There were costumes of every type. All at once, it was Mardi Gras and Halloween, and they were coming toward me.

I understood now, *the sea is giving up its dead. Giving up all those who gave up their lives while in her grasp.*

"B-e-w-a-r-e t-h-e d-a-y o-f t-h-e d-e-a-d," they were all mouthing the words.

I was cut off from reaching the Hummer. They were surrounding me like the gulls did, only they were not wanting dog food, they were wanting me. The only path they left for me to go, the only direction not barred by bodies, was into the sea. The ghoulish parade continued. I now had no choice but to walk into the gulf. They were prepared to push, drag, or knock me in that direction. I knew now the fate of the man who had left the note. I wondered how the man had been able to write a note surrounded by ghosts. Maybe he had known from some previous experience what was going to happen, or maybe he believed in the ancient ritual of the Aztecs.

Whatever it was, no one would ever know my own fate. They would find my Hummer abandoned, discover my despair at losing my precious Dee, and assume I had taken my own life.

As I entered the water, I saw a benign look on the faces of the souls around me. The water was cold, but somehow inviting. I waded deeper into the calm of the gulf. My knees, my waist, my chest, my shoulders, and then finally my head, too, were under the water. I became a ripple in the calm water with them. I had always been told that drowning was a terrible way to go, *but this is not so bad*, I thought

I was prepared to take my first breath of water; prepared to fill my lungs with the salty medium surrounding me replacing the life-giving oxygen. I remembered all the wrong I had done and asked whatever gods there were for forgiveness. When the saltwater entered my nose, it stung. When it got to my throat, I choked. I felt something tug at my leg as I prepared for the shock my lungs would receive when they filled with something other than air.

A fish must be trying to make a meal of me, I thought. *A shark, or barracuda, or something just as nasty.*

My lungs contracted, rejecting the salt water. I coughed out thinking that this was the last time I would do so, thinking I would swallow my tongue next, and then oblivion. I would join the others every year when the sea gives up victims on the day of the dead.

Then the voice returned, the voice and the tunnel vision.

Just as when he was a child, when he would lie in bed after his evening prayer – "Now I lay me down to sleep. I pray the Lord my soul to keep. If I should die before I wake, I pray the lord my soul to take" – occasionally, an eerie thing would happen, and he would be jolted awake on the verge of sleep, jolted by a voice, a loud voice almost screaming at him. It was then that the tunnel vision would occur. It seemed his body zoomed away into a far corner of the room and he would view the rest of his room as if through the opposite end of a pair of binoculars. Like the seagulls and their incessant squawking the voice would yell at him.

It was an out of body experience as if he were in a different world, one that was parallel to his own. He could see his other body but he looked down and could not see any part of the body he was now in. There were no hands, no feet, no arms, no legs, nothing attached to his eyes. In the morning his vision was back to normal and he had forgotten what the voice had said, but he remembered the strange phenomenon.

The tunnel vision and the tugging continued, only it was pushing him up. Pushing him up until he was above the surface of the gulf. He pulled air into his lungs, choking again as he breathed salt spray from a wave breaking over top of him. Finding himself a couple of feet above the water he was breathing air again and knew now that he would not drown. The tugging pulled him toward the shore while holding him up so he could breathe. His vision returned to normal and he felt sand under his feet again. He was able to walk the rest of the way, stumbling to his hands and knees as the weight of his wet clothing pulled him to earth.

Feeling something holding onto his legs, he looked down to see what he thought was seaweed. Trying to pull it off, he noticed that instead of seaweed, it was Portuguese Man of War tentacles, and they had stung him. When he had freed himself from the gelatinous material he crawled toward the Hummer turning once to look toward where he had almost lost his life.

There she was, standing up to her knees in the surf.

"Dee," he called out, "Dee, please don't leave me again!" He stood and tried to run toward her image, but she held up her hand to stop him. As he stood there watching, she returned to her watery grave.

He cried.

CHAPTER THREE

As a result of the stings from the jellyfish tentacles on the Day of the Dead, an infection developed. Portuguese man-of-war stings do not usually require hospitalization, but when the rash caused him to rub the areas raw, his leg became severely infected. He also had a reaction to the stings that caused difficulty breathing. On his way to Dallas, he stopped by the VA outpatient clinic in San Antonio and collapsed in the waiting area after giving the front desk clerk his name and last four digits of his SSN.

He awoke in a bed in a room that was obviously part of a hospital. He looked around with blurry eyes until he focused on a man in a wheelchair beside the bed watching TV. He tried to speak, but only a weak grunt came out.

"Unh," he said. The man turned around to face him.

"There ya'll are," he said. "Finally back from the dead after two days."

"Unh! Unh!" he said, trying to say two days. He tried to raise his right arm, but was unable to. His mind flashed back to El Dia de los Muertos, wondering if this was part of a dream.

"Let me get the doc," the man said, as he turned his wheelchair around and wheeled himself out of the room.

Looking around again, he saw an IV drip attached to his right arm. He tried to raise his arm, but it was tied down. This explained why he couldn't move it. His left arm felt as if it were tied down too.

"Doc's on the way," the man said as he wheeled back into the room. "You gave the staff here and at the outpatient clinic in San Antone a scare."

"Jellyfish sting," he was able to blurt out, remembering his encounter on Padre Island. His voice was starting to return, but it sounded gravelly like a cross between Andy Devine and Jack Palance. His throat hurt after he said the words. *Two days?* He wanted to ask, but couldn't.

"In case you was curious," the man continued with a Texas drawl, "you're at the VA hospital at Kerrville, north of San Antone, about sixty miles. They transported you here from the clinic there the day you collapsed in the lobby. You sure got their attention."

He understood the shortening of San Antonio that Texans seemed to always use.

A short Asian woman in a white hospital uniform entered the room with the ubiquitous stethoscope dangling from her neck.

"Hi, I'm Dr. Pica," she said. "How do you feel?"

"I don't know," he said, in that raspy voice. "I just woke up a couple of minutes ago. I feel tied down. Am I?" His ability to speak for longer periods was coming back to him.

"Yes, we had to put restraints on you so you wouldn't pull out your IV drip. We've had you on antibiotics since you arrived two days ago."

"What's ringing?" he asked. When he said this, both she and the man in the wheelchair had puzzled expressions.

"Oh, you may have some temporary tinnitus from the antibiotic," she said, smiling. Noticing his furrowed expression, she added. "Tinnitus is noise from your inner ear, usually ringing or buzzing. It should go away in a day or two." She started to remove his restraints. After she had him un-tethered, she raised the head of the bed.

"I'm really thirsty," he said.

The man in the wheelchair pulled a bottle of water from a pouch on the back of his chair, unscrewed the lid, and offered it to him.

"If'n ya don't mind drinkin' after me, ya kin have this water," he said.

"Don't mind at all," he said, taking the bottle gingerly with his left hand.

"I'll have the nurse bring you some of your own," Doctor Pica said.

He was in the center for almost a week, his ears still ringing, and was constantly visited by Tom, who was still in a wheelchair. Tom told him that his right ankle had been crushed during a boating accident. His left foot had slipped at the same time the boat had moved toward the pier pinning his foot between the two. Tom was to undergo surgery as soon as the swelling went down. They shared the common experience of having been on submarines, although Tom had been on an old diesel "pig" boat in the mid fifties and he had been on a missile carrying nuclear "boomer" sub in the late sixties. They swapped sea stories until he was discharged a week later. When Tom found out he had recently lost his wife, he decided to give his philosophical views of women.

"I was married five times, twice to the same woman," Tom said. "It's a good thing I ain't got much money, 'cause they all four wanted what little I did have when they left me. They fucked me comin' and goin'. I never had no kids and that might be why they took off when I couldn't knock 'em up. Turns out I have a low sperm count. Docs say it's from years of heavy smokin' and wearin' too tight a skivvies. I couldn't stand the government issue boxer trunks with the boys bouncin' around between my legs. So as soon's I got outa boot camp, I got me jockey shorts. I quit the smokin' years ago, but still wear the jockeys."

"I'm partial to jockeys too," he said. "I didn't know they could make you sterile, but that could be why I never had kids either." He left off the fact that he had never wanted any. He and Dee had never discussed it and she already had one child which satisfied him just fine. He was still on antihistamines and pain pills, so he let Tom philosophize as much as he wanted to.

"I have come to the conclusion," Tom said, "that no matter how good lookin' or ugly a woman is, beneath the fakaid still lies a woman."

He knew Tom meant façade, which would be quite a word coming from him. He decided that his friend must have read the word somewhere, didn't know how to pronounce it, and no one had corrected him so far. He wasn't about to be the first one to do so.

"Their minds are messed up from day one," he continued. "They're just like that there praying mantis that destroys their mate as soon's they get fertilized. That's all women want from a marriage is havin' babies. Once ya fulfill that obligation, they'd just as soon's not see ya again except to provide for them and their children, and sometimes not even then.

"Oh, they want their shoppin' money too. There's something that clicks on when they walk into a store. It makes 'em blind to price tags and anything practical such that they spend as if they have it ta spare.

"And they don't wanna fuck no more neither, 'cept ta father some more babies. Men just wanna fuck and women know it, so they lead us around like danglin' a carrot on a stick in front of a donkey. It's like they're holdin' that pussy out there where we can smell it.

"Then there's that menaphase thing when they go through the change. It's worse than the monthly curse ya put up with before the change. All we do is follow around hopin' we can get that carrot."

He felt sorry for Tom, who had obviously had bad luck with women. He had had a good woman in Dee, and missed her. He felt angry at not having been assertive enough to find a woman like her earlier in his life. He blamed it on the women he had known from his early childhood all the way through high school. One woman in particular whom he had nicknamed, "That Bitch." While lying in bed one night before he drifted off to sleep, he remembered how it was so long ago.

He was back in high school and felt terribly alone. Almost all his friends had dates and girlfriends. They passed notes in class, they ogled each other, they held hands between classes, they went to the favorite noon-time hangout for lunch together, they snuggled at the football games, they kissed. He had none of this and was afraid to even talk to a girl. So he just studied and thought about being lonely.

When he wanted to talk to someone in private, he had "the voice" to keep him company. The voice came with the tunnel vision when he seemed to zoom out from his body and hear a loud voice that almost shouted to him. The one episode with the voice that he had never forgotten brought back to life an event with That Bitch when they had exchanged Valentine's Day cards. They were both in the fifth grade and the card she had given to him had made him paranoid for life.

The voice called her "That Bitch," a name he whispered every time he saw her from then on.

So there he was, back in high school and at a football game. He was sitting in the last row in the top of the covered stands and That Bitch was with a group of boys and girls, all classmates, sitting five rows in front of him. He had been staring, trance-like, at them and her in particular, but not thinking of them. That Bitch turned around and saw him. She said something to the boy next to her and they started to laugh. Soon all of them turned around and started to laugh, making fun of him.

One of the boys got up and started towards him. As he approached, the boy took something from his jacket pocket. It was a small jar with liquid inside. By the time the boy got to the top row of seats, he was out of his trance-like stare and wanted to get up and leave. He looked to his right and one of the other boys was blocking the exit in that direction. When he turned back around the other boy had taken the lid off the small jar and splashed some of the liquid on him.

The smell was instantaneous and horrendous. He recognized it as Apple Blossom Perfume that sold in the local "tricks and jokes" store, the same place where exploding loads for cigarettes could be bought and other gag gifts. This was a real gag gift because those around him caught the scent. It was the smell of rotten eggs and soon everyone was telling him to leave the stands. He was getting angry at all of them. So angry he did not know what to do. The voice and his tunnel vision started. It somehow seemed out of place since he was not in the privacy of his bedroom.

Suddenly, he seemed to be viewing the scene as if he were not there. His viewing point was the back corner of the covered stadium, a place where no one sat unless the rest of the seats were taken. From his vantage point he could see them all in the distance, but they were not looking at him anymore. They were staring at an empty seat where he had been sitting. As if they did not understand where he had gone, the boy who had splashed him and the one guarding the exit ramp, went to where he had been. They looked around for him. He could see himself walking down the exit stairs between the wooden seats right past the boys almost touching them, but they apparently could not see him nor sense his presence.

This was the first time he had ever had the vision in a

public place.

This must be what happens around other people, he thought. *It's like I go to some parallel universe where I disappear temporarily.* As he watched himself heading toward the stadium exit, just as suddenly as he had zoomed out of his body, the world around him blurred as if he were traveling as fast as light. In an instant, he was back inside his own body and it stank terribly. He could barely stand the smell. Humiliated and depressed, he walked out of the stadium through the awful stares of those around him. It seemed no one took pity on him, so he walked home alone, dejected, and stinking.

He decided that night, that if he could, he was going to get even, not with the boys, because they were just doing what they felt lowered his status in the minds of all the girls. He was going to get even with the girls for not having any pity on him and not telling the boys to stop their ridicule.

His hospital friend, Tom, had been jilted many times, divorced by the same woman twice, and was bitter as hell about his experiences. Tom unloaded and talked for hours at a time about each one of them. In between his women stories, Tom would tell some genuinely interesting sea stories.

He was on antihistamines, antibiotics, and pain pills so he let Tom talk away. The only thing Tom said that was worth remembering was, "no matter how good looking, beneath the façade lies a woman." It took him awhile to realize that this was not meant to be flattering.

On the fourth day of antibiotics, he had again complained about his ringing ears. He was told again that it was probably the antibiotic and would stop as soon as he was taken off the medications. It didn't, and his hearing continued to get worse even though the infection and rash went away as his strength returned. On top of losing his hearing, the tunnel vision and voice from his childhood kept recurring. It was during one of these episodes that he was told what to do to erase the memories of the women from his past. It was to be like an exorcism of the demons of his past until they were all gone or he got caught. That Bitch would be the first to go.

His plan was laid out in his head while in the hospital. He had plenty of time while lying in bed and thought about what he was about to do as soon as he was released. By that time he was getting used to the ringing in his ears, but the loss of hearing was depressing. Doctor Pica finally came to the decision that his hearing loss might be permanent. She ordered him to visit the audiology department in the basement of the hospital.

After a couple of hours of testing, it was determined that he had possible nerve damage and high-frequency hearing loss. His hearing aid order was expedited and ten days later he had a new set of aids. Most of his hearing was restored, but it was not as good as it used to be.

After he was released, he set up the rent and utility accounts on his Corpus apartment so that they would be paid automatically. For dialing access to the internet, he purchased a better laptop and the software to connect the cell phone to the computer. The cell phones would be purchased along the way with a phony ID and paid for in cash and be discarded when the time was used up.

This time, he decided on a full-sized truck instead of a camper. A camper top, one he could sleep in when necessary, would be put on the bed of the truck. The sheltered bed of the truck would also serve as a traveling mortuary and dissection lab. Cardboard would be used to line the bed of the truck, to absorb any blood that might spill from the victims. Any blood that soaked through the cardboard could be easily washed off at a car wash. The Hummer he now owned would be left behind, parked in his apartment garage for later use.

He didn't need to go back to work as there was more than enough money from the lottery to carry out his plan.

CHAPTER FOUR

All I needed was the married names and addresses of the female classmates to carry out the exorcisms. The first to go would be "That Bitch," whose real name was Kate. I got her married name and address from a classmates website. The high school class reunion committee had someone who developed a meticulously kept site with names, addresses, some phone numbers, and pictures, old and recent, of all the known class members. It had been last updated in late 1997 after the thirty-fifth class reunion.

Years before the football game incident, there was my first humiliating encounter with That Bitch. She was the first girl I fell in love with, or whatever you can call love at ten years old, going on eleven. It was the fifth grade and we were in the same class in grade school. She was, to me, the prettiest girl in the entire world. The teacher had paired all the kids to work on an in-class assignment, and when I found out that she was my partner, I was thrilled. We sat together at the same wooden desk, but when she looked at me and said I had dirty ears, I was embarrassed and sickened all at the same time.

I used a handkerchief to wipe out my ears, one that crackled when I opened it. I had had a cold the last week and had not changed the hanky I used to blow my nose with. This made her back away even further than the sight of my dirty ears had just moments before. I wiped the left ear, the one facing her, and sure enough, the white, stained-yellow-with-snot kerchief came back coated with ear wax. I turned as red as a young boy could and would have returned to the sanctity of my own seat if I could have. I wiped the right ear with the same results. From that day on, I diligently cleaned my ears several times a day and made sure I had a clean handkerchief with me at all times.

Then I was presented with, what I considered, a way to make amends. We were to exchange Valentine's Day cards with other members of the class by drawing names from a hat. I got Kate's and found out that she also had gotten mine. I put a lot of time and effort into making the nicest card I could, but when we exchanged cards, my ego and feelings were hurt even more deeply than after the dirty-ear episode.

"Yuck!" she had written on the inside of the card. It was underlined in red ink, followed by three exclamation points, and in bigger letters than the "Be Mine" message printed on the opposite page. I could have crawled into a hole with a thousand snakes and not felt any worse. That Bitch!

I pulled in at the Best Value Motel on Pike Street adjacent to I-77. Formulating my plan would take me at least a week and three trips to Marietta, staying in a different place each time, paying cash, and using an alias. I had several different drivers' licenses with different names on them which I had made on my computer. The phony licenses wouldn't fool a cop, but I wasn't going to use the phony ones if I had a run-in with the law. I also used different license plates that I had amassed in the past year, all from different states. It was easy to take the front plate from a car, especially in states where only a rear one was required. I could also make temporary tags if needed. Local motel owners didn't know the rules in other states concerning required expiration stickers and whether both a front and rear plate were required. I simply changed plates at a rest stop late at night along an interstate highway. I made damn sure I didn't break any traffic laws in and around the towns I was scoping out. I also stayed only a day or two each time, to lessen the chance of getting noticed. It wasn't unusual for someone from out of state to be in town on vacation or a holiday, and I used this to my advantage.

Anyone who has attended a high school reunion can attest to the fact that facial features change over several years. It helped that I had the most recent class reunion group photo to use from the website. That Bitch had been to the one last year, so I was armed with a fairly recent representation of what she looked like. I must admit that she had not changed much over the course of thirty years and still could be considered attractive. Gone were the big glasses that were prevalent back in the early sixties, probably replaced by contact lenses or lasik surgery.

I connected my laptop to my cell phone and did an internet search using Cyber Detective, which can provide a lot of information about someone, like where they worked, where they lived, their telephone number, marriage status, criminal records, etc. The only piece of information I could glean from my search was a verification of That Bitch's address, and that would prove to be enough. I re-verified the address in the local phone book and did a drive-by to get a feel for the neighborhood.

Across the road from her house were woods with lots of trees to hide behind. It was an ideal location for scouting the house. Along the edge of the woods were several blackberry thickets which could easily be penetrated in the winter. I returned to my motel and turned in early to get a good night's sleep. I would be up way before dawn and heading to the woods to set up an observation post. That night I dreamed of my past, a past I had retreated from after I met Dee, when I had gotten a second chance at life.

The reason I had started killing women before I fell in love with Dee the first time I met her was not entirely clear to me. It was as if someone else were doing the murders while I observed. I was able to reverse all the wrongs I had done, meet Dee under different circumstances, and start a new life all because of a boat named *The Fisher Cat* and a captain who went by the name of John Potter, or as he liked to be called, Cap'n Johnny.

The Fisher Cat was accursed, but I considered the curse a blessing. A gypsy woman from New Orleans, angry with the pirates who had killed her husband while they were out at sea, had used some voodoo magic to put a spell on the boat, just before she had jumped overboard and drowned herself to escape further torture and certain death at the hands of the same pirates. Whenever the boat got a few miles away from the shore the curse caused it to be transported back in time. As it approached shore it always returned to the present as if nothing had happened.

The captain knew about the spell, and I had hired him to take me out to sea. On one of our trips back in time, I was able to abandon ship before the boat came to shore. I remained in the time warp while Cap'n Johnny, his boat, and a cat of mine whom I had named Dedra after Dee's daughter, returned to the present. I found myself left in a time just before I had started the serial killings.

I knew where Dee lived and was able to meet her again, only she didn't know who I was this time or, that one of my victims had been her daughter. Of course when we met this time her daughter was very much alive, as were all the others. The same chemistry between us that had evolved while I was on the murder spree was there, and she fell in love with me all over again. We had a wonderful life until she and her daughter took the flight to Paris and disappeared forever. In an effort to try and travel back in time, back to before Dee boarded the plane and thus stop her, I tried to find Cap'n Johnny, but he was no where to be found. I assumed that on one of his trips back in time, he had met some ill fate and therefore, no longer existed.

The dream was of the murders before they were erased by time travel. I had taken my drugged and blood-drained victims to my mansion on a mountain top in Vermont, dismembered them, and fed parts of them to my cats. I had acquired one new cat for each victim, giving the cat the victim's name. After cutting them up into smaller pieces, I then froze the remaining parts of their bodies for later consumption. The scene in my "cutting room" played over and over again until I awoke with a start at four thirty.

"Time to get this show started," I said aloud, to no one.

There was no time to shower, only to drain my dragon and don some dark green jeans and a brown denim jacket, clothes I thought would blend in well with the autumn/winter-like colors of the woods. It was warm this January, so I didn't need to bundle up to protect myself from the cold weather. Camouflage clothes would have been better, but I needed to walk the two miles, some of which was in the open, to the woods across from That Bitch's house and did not want to draw attention to myself. I took along an MP3 player loaded with David Baldacci's audio book, *The Winner*, which would stave off the boredom while I was stalking my prey. The story was about a lottery winner, which reminded me of my own luck with the lottery. Some jerky and a bottle of Propel sport drink would abate some of my hunger and thirst.

When I reached the woods I hadn't passed a single soul. It was five thirty in the morning by the time I settled in across from the house. Perching on a slight rise allowed me to look down on the front of the house and with the binoculars I could actually see in through the dining room window. By six, lights in the houses started to be turned on up and down the street. A girl delivering papers sped along the sidewalk on an electric scooter, tossing the daily newspaper onto front porches with uncanny accuracy.

At six fifteen, a light appeared in the dining room window, not a light from that room, but a beam of indirect light which must have been coming from a kitchen area near the back of the house. After just enough time had past to start a pot of coffee, the front porch light came on, and a man dressed in a wine colored robe and blue slippers, opened the front door and bent down to retrieve the paper. He was bald, a bit fat, and about the right age to be That Bitch's husband.

Just as he closed the door, I felt the hairs on the back of my neck stand on end. I had the feeling of being watched. I turned slowly around and was face to face with a cat. It was a thin cat with brown, gray, and black markings and looked like Dedra, the cat in my dreams; the one I had with me when I was chased from my mansion in Vermont; the one I took with me on the Fisher Cat; and the one left with Cap'n Johnny when I abandoned ship. The cat was staring at me with those red eyes. The eyes I had seen so many times in my dreams.

"Here kitty," I whispered.

The cat did not move, nor did it unlock its eyes from mine. Reaching into my jacket pocket and pulling out a piece of jerky, I offered some to the cat. It still did not move so I set the piece of jerky on the ground at arm's distance from me off to my right side so I could detect motion around it. I turned back to the house as slowly as I could so I wouldn't startle my visitor. Although I had just noticed it, the cat could have been there for some time before I had felt its gaze. Not having my hearing aids in and listening to the audio book caused me to miss any noise the cat might have made. If it were a stray and living in the woods, it would not have made much noise anyway. It would be constantly in a stealth mode, stalking for prey. My hearing was bad, but at least I had good peripheral vision, and if the cat got curious about the piece of jerky, out of the corner of my right eye I would be able to detect it. It stayed where it was, still leery of this human who wasn't afraid, nor threatening. I continued watching the house and listening to the audio book.

At eight o'clock, the garage door opened and a green Cadillac Escalade became visible. *They're doing all right*, I thought. *There's a car worth fifty grand*. It puzzled me why someone living in Southern Ohio wanted an SUV, although I had seen a lot of them in Florida too, owned, no doubt, by people who never drove anywhere four-wheel drive was needed. In the garage, next to the Escalade, was a RAV4, another SUV, although much more practical than the Caddy.

As the Escalade backed out and to my right, I could see through the windshield and driver's side window that the driver was the same man who had picked up the paper two hours ago. He had on a suit coat and a tie, looking like a banker or lawyer. He reached up to his right and must have pushed the closer for the garage door which started to descend as he pulled away. He dropped his hand and picked up a cup from the cup holder and raised it to his mouth.

In my concentration and because the binoculars had blocked my peripheral vision, I forgot about the piece of jerky I had left for the cat. When I glanced toward where I had put it, the cat was sitting in place of the jerky cleaning its face with the back of its paw. It stopped when it noticed I was looking, but resumed its cleaning when it decided I wasn't a threat. It did watch me intently as I reached into my jacket pocket and produced another piece of dried meat. This time when I held it out, it leaned in my direction and gently grabbed the proffered morsel with its mouth.

While I continued my observation, the cat took two more

pieces of meat, but never moved closer than my outstretched arm.

Two more chapters of the audio book ended before there was any more activity from That Bitch's house. This time when the garage door went up, the RAV4 backed out and turned the same way as the Escalade had. There was a woman behind the wheel and although she had aged a bit, it was unmistakably That Bitch. She headed towards the end of the street, made a right-hand turn and disappeared down the street, hidden by the houses. Before she returned, I had listened to three more chapters.

While listening to the book, I had watched the comings and goings on the street. The mail was delivered to the brick mailboxes along the street. Gone were the days when all the mail was delivered on foot right up to the house. Some small towns still did so, but in most new housing areas the post office required boxes on the street. I had lived in one such community in a suburb of Dallas, where the kids took delight in blowing the top off the brick mailboxes using a combination of homemade explosives.

"Topping," they called it. When it had happened to my neighbor's mailbox, the post office was nice enough to hold his mail until the box was repaired which was a bigger inconvenience than the two-hundred dollars it cost him to fix it. I had been luckier in that I had found a half-burned paper bag of men's hair gel in mine. I called the cops because I didn't know what the hell it was. They actually sent out a bomb squad to clean up the mess. I wasn't so lucky when my box was pushed over, another game they called "rocking," descriptive of the way that they rocked the brick mail box assembly back and forth until it toppled. When I had it replaced, I had pins put in the sidewalk to keep it from being rocked again.

That Bitch had an easy license plate to memorize. It was personalized with her first name, K8S KAR. Cute, and I wouldn't have to write it down. Of course it stood for "Kate's car," using the eight to replace "ate." It should have been THT BTCH.

While That Bitch was gone, I explored the hill I was hiding on and found a back way out. There was another road to the west that only had a couple of houses on it. I could leave my lookout post before dark without being seen and thus not raise any suspicion. I also observed the neighbors' routines, but they were not much of threat because of the distance between houses.

Three more days of observation verified that the man of the house left precisely at 8:00 every weekday morning. That Bitch's comings and goings varied, which made me believe that she was not going to a job of any sort. Once she returned with plastic bags on the seat of the RAV4 with a loaf of French bread sticking out. Before I could tell for sure what was in the bags, she had closed the garage door. Satisfied I had all the information I needed to do the job, I just needed to wait for a dark, overcast day so that, while she was gone. With less chance of being seen, I could gain access to the house.

Each day that I was there, the cat came out to get some food and I made sure to have enough for both of us. I was going to miss my companion when my job was finished.

CHAPTER FIVE

It was a rare snow day in southeastern Ohio, just the type of day that I needed for cover. After observing the weather forecast, I left my keys and a small tip for the cleaning lady in the room and left the motel at four in the morning. The night before, I had paid for my room in advance, so there was no need to stop by the office. If everything went as planned, I would be gone from the area by mid afternoon. If an opportunity to enter the house did not present itself, I would return on another day, staying in a different place. I had a good feeling that this was the day and ironically it was VD, Valentines Day. This cupid would shoot more than an arrow into That Bitch's heart.

I drove my truck to a parking lot that I had previously picked for its closeness to a major road leading out of Marietta and for the number of parking places that were secluded enough that my truck would not be observed carrying out the second phase of my plan. The lot was also within walking distance of That Bitch's house and on the backside of my observation hill. White snow pants, a white down-filled jacket, white gloves, and a white stocking cap made me nearly invisible in the heavy snow that had started to fall around four fifteen. A white colored fabric work bag held all the tools I would need.

Even though I was in a different location on the hillside from where I had previously observed the house, as soon as I squatted down, the friendly cat appeared. I fed it this time from a can of cat food I had picked up at the convenience store where I had filled the truck with gasoline the night before. The cat ate every bit of the food and started cleaning itself as That Bitch's husband pulled out of the garage. He was early this morning, probably because of the snowfall and worsening driving conditions. That Bitch might not even leave the house today, but she had every other day I had been here and I expected snow would not stop her. Her RAV4, being all-wheel drive, could navigate almost as easily as my four-wheel drive truck.

Right after I peeled back the lid from the second can of food and gave it to the cat, the garage door opened, and That Bitch backed the RAV4 out of the drive and headed to the north. I waited until a particularly heavy squall of snow started falling providing me cover with nearly white-out conditions. This urged me from my observation point to start phase two.

Leaving my observation spot after saying good-by to my friend, I headed down the hill. I crossed the road heading toward the side of the house where the telephone wires ran down from the electrical drop and into the house. Just in case there was a burglar alarm, I opened my bag, took out a pair of wire cutters and cut the wires, thus preventing the system from dialing an outside number. It was a chance I had to take that the phone line was not monitored.

Had the phone lines connected to the alarm panel been monitored, the alarm company would receive a signal that the line was severed. The company would then call the home number to verify that the line was no longer connected. They would then go down the list of alternate numbers, which, most likely, would include That Bitch's cell phone, a neighbor, and That Bitch's husband's work number and cell phone. The weather could be considered the reason the phone line was no longer working, but that was an assumption I could not rely upon. Therefore, I was taking a chance that these, like most lines, were not monitored.

If there was an alarm system, I wanted to enter through a door that had an alarm delay. A delayed-entry door allowed someone with the correct code a set time period, usually sixty seconds, to disarm the system. The delay would give me some time to locate the alarm panel and disable the siren. If I did not find the panel before the alarm sounded, I would try to find the horn. The noise would not carry very far in the howling wind and I should have lots of time to disable it.

After cutting the phone wire, I went to the window in the side of the garage. No alarm systems I knew of had motion detectors in the garage. The window did not have glass breakage detection or alarm sensors attached to it. I could, therefore, safely assume it was not armed. Using a suction cup and a glass cutter, I made a small hole in the single-pane glass, large enough to reach through to unlatch the locks. I opened the window and slipped into the empty garage. From my observation point up on the hill, I had noticed how clean and neat the garage was. There was nothing but a few garden implements, trash cans, and two bicycles arranged neatly along the walls. With some clear packing tape I put the removed piece of glass back in its place to keep snow from blowing in and alerting That Bitch when she pulled into the garage. I then headed for the door leading into the house. I took off my heavy gloves and put on a pair of latex gloves to preclude leaving a set of fingerprints. I removed all of my snow clothing and piled it behind the trash barrel in the corner of the garage.

I pried loose the upper door stop enough to slip a piece of sheet metal between the top part of the door and the header jamb. If there was a door alarm, it would be in this location. When I opened the door, the piece of metal would keep the magnetic sensor from detecting an open door and leave the alarm un-tripped. This also worked on button-type sensors too. Defeating the door alarm would buy me a little more time to locate the alarm panel. The door leading from the garage into the house was unlocked, which is what most people do when they have a garage door opener, so I carefully pushed the door open.

Feeling the top of the door I found the embedded alarm sensor. I carefully opened the door enough so I could squeeze through. I then dropped down on my hands and knees and crawled through the house to avoid setting off the motion sensors. Most sensors have large-animal dead zones to avoid false alarms when Fido is home by himself. There was a motion sensor in the upper left corner of the room I had just crawled into from the garage and an arm/disarm panel was on the opposite wall. I made my way along the floor keeping low and moving as slowly as I could. When I got to the hallway where a second arm/disarm panel was located, I saw that there were no motion sensors, so I was able to stand up. I saw a pull-down ladder in the ceiling which must lead to the crawl space above the main living areas. That is where most main alarm panels and their horns are placed in houses without basements. The absence of cellar windows indicated that there was no basement. Pulling the door open, I slid the ladder down, and went up into the attic area. There was a cord hanging down and I pulled it. A light came on and I quickly located the alarm panel attached to a roof support column.

Locating the horn wire, I cut it first and then I cut all the other signal wires leading into the panel even though this was not necessary. Opening the panel and disconnecting the battery and power supply completely disabled the system. This phase done, I could sit back and await my prey. That Bitch would notice that the alarm did not beep as soon as she opened the garage door, but a lot of people forget from time to time to arm their systems when they leave the house. Absent any visible sign of forced entry she would not be concerned. I returned to the door where I had entered, removed the piece of steel from the doorsill and cleaned up any indication that the door had been tampered with.

With nothing else to do until That Bitch returned, I decided to take a nap in a chair next to the garage hoping the sound of the garage door opening would awaken me. I pulled out my stun gun and set it on the stand next to me.

I dreamt.

I was walking on a lonely country road, a road with two dirt-filled ruts and gravel pushed up on the sides and middle. It was a dry and dusty road now, but must have been nearly impassible when it rained.

It could rain today, I thought, for the sky was overcast and grey. There was a split-rail fence lining the road to my right surrounding a field of short grass, but there was nothing else in that field, no trees, no cows, no horses, nothing but grass. There was no evidence such as "meadow muffins" indicating that any farm animals had been there. There was also no sign that the field had been planted recently or even last season, as there were no corn stalks or soy plants scattered about from fallen seed.

On my left was another field, this one with only fifty feet of grass and then underbrush which stretched out beyond onto a small rise. In the distance on the right and in front were hills dotted with trees. I could see an old log cabin off in the distance on the right.

I kept walking. I was wearing a heavy coat which I called my "puffy coat," the one with the hood I seldom used and with the front zipper that came to the top of the collar so I could cocoon myself all the way to the top of my chin. My puffy coat was reserved for only the harshest winter days when I had lived in Vermont. I was wearing gloves too, but my uncovered head felt neither cold nor warmth. Had I put this coat on for a walk in the country on a spring or summer day?

Taking off the gloves, I stashed them in one of the four front pockets, and unzipped the coat. I was wearing a heavy sweatshirt underneath, the one with the purple and white RAIDERS letters across the front. Looking past the fleeced-lined blue jeans I was wearing, I saw that I also had on the heavy work boots I had bought for cutting and splitting logs when I had lived on the top of the mountain in Vermont.

There was something moving on my back and I felt something cold on the back of my ear. I reached up and behind and felt the fur of an animal. It mewed softly as I touched it and immediately I knew it was my cat, Dedra; the one I had left on the boat with Cap'n Johnny. I tried to say her name. My lips moved, but I made no noise. I tried to repeat it, with the same results.

Maybe I've gone completely deaf, I thought. *Maybe I am saying the words but can't even hear or feel the vibrations coming from my throat.*

I didn't have time to ponder this before it started to rain. Just a sprinkle, but the sky looked ominous off to my right. Clouds rolled in and I started to look for someplace I could get to before the clouds let loose a flooding torrent as they were now threatening. Dedra moved to my shoulder expressing her discomfort as the sprinkle turned into a steady downpour. When I reached around to get her to put her under my coat in front as I had done many times before, I felt her arch under my touch. She made a loud reroew sound just as a bolt of lightening struck the hillside in front of us.

Hail started to fall and I stumbled to my left as if slipping on something. I reached out with my right hand bracing for a fall and closed my eyes to shield them from the stinging pellets.

Recovering from the near fall, he opened his eyes to see snow, not rain or mud, but snow all around him. He blinked, but there was still snow and it was coming down hard. The view was also far away and distorted. *Tunnel vision*, he thought.

Now he felt cold, so he zipped up his puffy coat and pulled his gloves out of his pocket. He remembered the cat and reached around to comfort her but she was not in his hood. Thinking she had fallen, He quickly turned around and saw nothing but snow.

"Dedra," he called, but she was not there. Perplexed, he looked around then suddenly knew where he was. He was on a familiar road in Vermont, one he had jogged on in the summer and one he had hiked along to pick up the newspaper that was delivered a quarter mile down the road. The field that was there before had changed to woods, the split-rail fence was a stone wall, and it was snow coming down instead of rain. He put on the gloves and pulled the hood up over his head.

My dream ended with the sound of the garage door opening. I grabbed the stun gun and got up waiting in the darkness on the other side of the entrance to the garage. A car pulled into the garage and the garage door started to close. The car door opened and I heard the rustling of bags and then the car door slammed shut. My heart was racing from not only the anticipation, but the effects of the dream.

The door opened and she walked in, obviously struggling with some heavy packages and a purse over one arm. She walked into the room and headed toward the kitchen. I was right behind her. When she sensed someone was there and started to turn around, I zapped her with almost a million volts, enough to knock down a horse. She collapsed immediately taking the groceries and her purse to the floor with her. I grabbed a hypodermic from my bag along with a vial of sodium pentobarbital, a paralyzing drug used by veterinarians when euthanizing animals. I produced another vial, this time of potassium chloride, and found a suitable vein in her arm in which to inject it.

Had she been fully conscious, she would have felt the

burning in her veins as I injected the drug. The searing pain would extend all the way to the heart where it would cause the heart to stop beating and she would be dead in less than five minutes. Had I used pancuronium, a drug to paralyze the diaphragm, before I injected the potassium chloride, I would have been using the same method administered by states that execute condemned prisoners by lethal injection. Pancuronium is hard to get, therefore I had to shortcut the procedure.

I sat back on the floor after the second injection and waited. After two minutes, I felt for a pulse and got none. Phase two was over.

Sitting back down on the floor with my back against the wall, I admired my handiwork. That Bitch was gone forever, if not from my mind, at least from this earth. I shrugged off the thought that maybe someone would miss a wife, a friend, a mother, or a grandmother. She had played a part in making me what I am today, and she had to pay.

Paid in full, I thought, *but not quite yet*. I rummaged through her purse and produced a ring of keys, one of which looked like an ignition key. It had the sombrero looking hat symbol that Toyota uses, so I knew I had the RAV4 keys.

I opened the door to the garage and walked to the hatchback on the RAV4. It had tinted windows, which would ensure no one could see in as I drove away with the body inside. I opened the door and saw more groceries held in place by a cargo net. They would remain and I would use them to further hide That Bitch. The rear seats were already folded forward and down so there was plenty of room.

Returning to the house, I grabbed That Bitch by the arms and dragged her to the back of the RAV4. I took out the groceries, hoisted the body into place, and retrieved my snow clothes. I piled the groceries and snow clothes around the body, and closed the hatchback.

A movement caught my eye at the garage window. Looking toward it, I saw my cat friend peering in at me.

"Well, look who's here," I said aloud. I re-entered the house and retrieved my tool bag. I then went back to the garage closing the door behind me. I looked over and saw the cat still peering in at me, meowing and pawing at the window.

What the hell, I thought. *I'll let her into the house and she can spend a warm afternoon before all hell breaks loose.* Opening the window just enough for the cat to crawl through, I let her in. She started rubbing my legs, first with her jaws, which contained the scent sacs, and then with the side of her body. I closed the window and she followed me as I went to the door to the house and opened it. The cat had no intention of going inside, but when I closed the door and headed toward the driver's side door, she followed.

I opened the door and, to my surprise, the cat jumped in.

"Well, if you want to come along, I guess it's all right," I said to the cat. It meowed and took a seat on the passenger's side, sitting up as if to say, "What are we waiting for?" I pulled a piece of jerky from my pocket and tossed it on the passenger seat. The cat sniffed it, looked up as if to say thanks, and then started chewing on the piece of dried meat without taking it off the seat. I glanced at my other passenger, tossed my tool bag on top of her, and got in. After banging my knees on the dash, I moved the seat back, and started the car. The cat didn't even look up, intent on chewing the stringy meat. I closed the car door, pushed the button on the remote garage door opener, and looked over my right shoulder.

When the garage door had nearly completed its ascent, I started backing out and down the drive.

"Phase three underway," I said to my feline passenger. I pulled slowly away from the house, making sure the garage door closed all the way. There was another snow squall swirling around the neighborhood creating a whiteout condition.

All the better to keep me from being seen, I thought. *Us*, I corrected as I glanced at the cat.

When I got to the lot where my truck was waiting, it was still snowing heavily. The snow would mask my tire tracks, the RAV4, and what I had to do next. Rather than pull into the spot next to my truck, I stopped behind it so that the hatchback of the RAV4 was even with the right side of my truck. The truck and RAV4 would shield anyone on two sides from seeing me move That Bitch from one vehicle to the other. The other two sides faced the back and the hilly sides of the lot. With the snow as cover I could work without being detected. Getting out of the RAV4 I hit the unlock switch on my truck key ring, disarming both the cab and camper top alarms. I then unlocked the hatch to the top part, opened it, and pulled the tailgate down.

I opened the hatchback, gave the surroundings a quick look, and pulled That Bitch out, sliding her up and into the truck. As if on cue, the cat bounded into the back of the RAV4, skirted the grocery bags, and leaped into the back of the pickup.

"I guess you're in it for the long run," I said. I took the groceries, my snow clothes, and my work bag from the RAV4 and placed them in the pickup. I then closed the hatchback and the tailgate but left the camper-top hatch door open. "I'll be back shortly," I said to the cat who was peering out the back of the pickup. I drove the RAV4 to another place in the lot, got out, locked it, and returned to the camper top of the pickup, crawled inside and closed the hatch behind me latching it from the inside. The cat was still there, sniffing around that Bitch's corpse.

Having completed phase three, I was now ready to move on to phase four. This phase would be modified from what I had originally planned because of the entry of the cat, my feral cat, onto the scene. I could have referred to her as homeless, but she now had a home and seemed to enjoy it since she did not run away even when given every opportunity to do so. I used the term "feral" only in the sense that she had been on her own until she happened on me in the woods. For all I knew, she might have belonged to someone in That Bitch's neighborhood; however, she chose to be with me and I was not going to kick her out. She was free to go whenever she got tired of me and my travels across the country. She also had seemed quite happy to assist me in the completion of phase four.

The chunk of That Bitch's heart removed by my feral cat, I was now almost ready for phase five. There were only two more phases to go before I moved on to my second revenge. I was going to plant evidence on That Bitch's body, something she deserved and would forever stay with her into the next life, or eternity. I had obtained the evidence from a dog, a stray. But unlike my feral cat, the dog had not been so fortunate. I had kept the evidence cold and in an ice chest so that there would be no spoilage. I wanted law enforcement to find fresh evidence attesting to That Bitch's status in life, spelled out in the coded message I would leave.

The evidence was in a syringe with the needle removed. Not a surgical syringe, but one of the type used for basting turkeys. The cat was watching me intently but was also busy cleaning her paws and wiping her face after having helped me in phase four. The "lunch" she had just eaten as part of phase four was a bit messy, and I had let her have as much as she wanted. She had only taken a few bites so what remained was still identifiable.

After injecting the contents of the basting needle into That Bitch in two distinct places, I tossed the syringe back into the ice chest to be disposed of along with any other evidence. After opening the two sliding windows, I crawled back into the cab of the truck followed closely by the cat. There was a boot between the truck and the rear part, so snow and rain could not get in. I shut the sliding windows, got into the driver's seat and started the truck. It was still snowing heavily so that my tracks would be covered by snowfall within minutes. As I exited the parking lot after driving by That Bitch's parked car, I saw a snow plow beginning to work at clearing the lot. The plow was starting at the far side of the lot away from where I had pulled out.

Good! I thought. Any tracks left by my truck would be removed completely erasing any sign of my having been here. They might even plow a pile of snow behind That Bitch's car further hiding it from view, adding to the snow which had already piled up on the horizontal surfaces.

The cat took up a place riding shotgun

"I think I'll name you Dedra, after a cat I used to have back in another place and time," I said to the cat, who meowed as if in acceptance, if not approval.

Phase four and five completed, I headed south toward West Virginia. Now onto phases six and seven, the last two parts of my plan. I pushed the auto-four-wheel drive button, just in case it was needed. The snow reminded me of the dream.

Chapter Six

Four days after I had taken That Bitch to the parking lot, I arrived at the desolate place in the country I had earlier selected. The weather had warmed up overnight, and the bags of ice I had packed around her body, still in the back of the truck, were starting to melt. The snow base was also melting quickly so that by afternoon it would be nearly all gone. That was the way snow happened in southern Ohio. It was here one day and gone less than a week later.

"Husband Not A Suspect," read the headlines of yesterday's *Marietta Times* lying on the passenger seat. Dedra was asleep on the seat in the extended cab on the passenger's side. "Struggle evident at home of missing housewife," read the sub-headline. The article went on to report that the security system had been disabled and that her husband had found the groceries scattered about the kitchen. He had been on a business trip for three days, which was unexpected on my part. Therefore, I was compelled to hang around in West Virginia a lot longer than I had planned. The headline in the paper was what I was waiting for so that I could dump the body just before I called the police to report its location.

Had I dumped the body right away, animals might have destroyed the crime scene before the authorities had time to respond and would have ruined my fun. Now with a known missing person in the area, law enforcement would take a call more seriously and respond a lot more quickly. I then prepared the note with her blood and deposited the other evidence which would provide the local yokels something to play with. Before I headed to my next destination, I wanted to observe how the police reacted to what I had done to the body of That Bitch. After I left, I planned on monitoring the investigation progress by using key-word searches on the internet. At least I would be able to observe for a while until the media moved on to more important issues.

After going back across the Ohio River, I pulled onto an isolated road off Route 60 making sure the truck was not visible from the main road. This would be my dump site, which I had picked because there was a suitable observation point at the top of a hill, on the opposite side of the road, about a mile away. From there I could view those who would find the body. Stopping the truck, I offered to let Dedra out, but she was content to lie on the seat and let me do the dirty work. After a careful check around to make sure no one was watching me, I opened the back of the truck and slid That Bitch's body toward me by pulling on the cardboard she was resting on. The heart, which had been removed in phase four, was slipped into my coat pocket. Hoisting the stiff body onto my shoulder, I headed for the side of the road about one-hundred feet away from the truck.

I tossed That Bitch onto the ground at my feet and placed the heart next to her. From another coat pocket I pulled out the note that I had made especially for her and placed it on her chest.

"That looks pretty good," I said stepping back and admiring the arrangement before me. A nearby rock was used to keep the note from blowing away. Gloves kept me from leaving fingerprints on the rock, or any other surface. Returning to my truck, I left the area by continuing on the dirt road until it circled back around to Route 60. At the top of a small hill, my cell phone indicated a good signal so I proceeded to call Sheriff Dag. The cell phone had been bought with cash in a different store from the calling card. I had used an alias to activate the phone. I had no intention of using it more than once. After I was finished with the phone I would take the battery out. The phone, minus the battery, along with everything else I had worn or used on this trip, was going to be consumed in a bonfire. The bags the ice had been in, every piece of cardboard in the back of the pickup, and anything else that might lead to me as a suspect would go in the fire. Fire was a wonderful destroyer of evidence, which I had found out a few years before. Tossing the ashes from the fire into a toilet ensured nothing could be linked back to me. Because the cell-phone battery might explode in a fire, I would toss it into a dumpster somewhere to be taken to a landfill and buried for eternity.

As an extra security measure, I dialed the long distance credit card number from the cell phone and punched in the card number. The call recipient, if they had caller ID, would see a location somewhere in Utah as the origination point. The call could never be traced to me. I dialed the next set of numbers from memory.

"Sheriff Dag," the answerer said. The only thing he heard was the description of a location and the words, "found body hunting." I then hung up. I proceeded to my lookout perch on the opposite side of the road from That Bitch's body where I waited, Dedra by my side. If no one came soon, I would repeat the call until they did.

CHAPTER SEVEN

BACK IN COLUMBUS, HOMICIDE detective Ginny Joynt had just sat down at her computer with her second cup of coffee for the day. Her first had been from a Starbuck's on her way to the precinct. This second one was not nearly as good, but it would have to do. She avoided looking to her left where Detective Joe Palosi, the man who made the coffee each morning, was sitting. He was a veteran of the force with thirty years of service and just counting the days, not just figuratively either. He announced the number of days each morning to the grunts of his fellow co-workers. He reminded Ginny of her great grandfather, a right-off-the-boat Italian who had brought his crude up-bringing across the sea with him. She hoped she had inherited her great grandfather's genes, because he lived to be 105 years old, dying in his sleep one night while she was still in high school.

It seemed Joe's toughest assignment was to make coffee in the huge urn they used for the entire office and then clean out the pot at the end of the day. Just before he went home, he would sit at his desk and wipe the coffee grounds from his hairy arms. He even saved the used grounds and took them home with him at the end of the day.

"For my compost pile," he would announce, to anyone who noticed him carrying the bag of grounds out the door.

She tried to avoid the spectacle by being away from her desk when his time to go home neared, but once in awhile she had to endure his one-man circus. One morning he had entertained her by showing her the plum tomato someone had given him.

"I think I'll get the seeds from this one," he had said, holding the tomato up so all who wanted to see could, "for my garden." He had then proceeded to smash the tomato on his desk blotter and roll the mess back and forth, pausing between rolls to pick out the seeds one by one. She had avoided telling him that the seeds used to grow that tomato probably came from a hybrid and what he had so carefully harvested from the mashed tomato would not yield good plants.

"Seventy-two days," he declared.

Thank God, she thought. *I just hope my sanity lasts that long.*

"You ain't gonna believe this," her boss, Captain Clark Barr said, scaring her half out of her wits and causing her to spill a little coffee from the cup in her right hand. He had come up behind her while she was shielding her peripheral vision from the Joe Palosi circus on her left.

"Believe what?" she asked, recovering quickly.

"The autopsy report on the body down in Devola," he answered. "First, it did confirm that her name was Kate E. Bardydohr. Second, there was some DNA, not hers, found in her vagina and anus. Third, it was semen. Fourth, it was not human semen."

Everyone in the room was now facing in their direction.

"Not human?" she said, reluctantly playing along with his count-down game. "What type was it?"

"The corner doesn't know for sure until he checks with

a vet," he went on, "but he suspects it to be canine. You know, from a dog."

She knew what canine meant, but was so appalled by the idea that someone had a dog hump a victim, she didn't respond immediately.

"I know what you're thinking," he went on. "The report is stating that from the way it was deposited, the semen appears to have been implanted. It was all in one place, one wad, so to speak, and all the sperm was dead when it was inserted."

"That is so disgusting," she heard herself say. She regretted it the second after the words had come out, but it had been said and couldn't be taken back. The others were thinking the same thing, so her concerns that the others might think her a weak woman were unfounded.

"We're going to hold back that little piece of information as something only the killer would know. It also would hurt the family of the victim if they heard that now while grieving. So," he raised his voice for all to hear, "this bit of evidence does not leave this room." He looked around as if making a mental note of each person's reaction and who was listening.

"What about the numbers?" she asked, wanting desperately to get the thought of dog semen from her mind. She knew, however, that the thought would not go away.

"I turned that over to Jim Yerblood," he said. "He has the experience to decipher the message and will be working with you on this case."

Jim spent most of his spare time doing puzzles. He could complete the most difficult Sudoku in just under ten minutes. During his unscheduled coffee breaks, he loved to play with cryptograms on the puzzle page of the daily newspaper. He met monthly with other math aficionados to discuss unsolvable math problems such as the Goldbach Conjecture, the Riemann Hypothesis, and the Hadamard matrix. His gift for solving puzzles carried over into his speech mannerisms and he would sometimes say things that were a mix of metaphors.

When she had first met him he had told her, "Your name is familiar, but your face don't ring a bell." She had shaken his hand and walked away while the detectives that were in the room with him all snickered. She thought him good looking and tall, but he had other mannerisms that turned her off. The fact that he had been married in civil ceremonies twice and divorced three times, spoke volumes about him. His third wife had been by common law, which was a valid marriage and had required a divorce. His first wife had caught him cheating on her, divorced him, and turned him in to the local draft board reporting that he no longer had a "married" exemption. He was immediately drafted into the Marines and sent to Vietnam, where he had almost lost a leg in a Vietcong ambush. Most of his platoon had been killed, but he had survived with a bullet wound that had become gangrenous. Instead of amputating, the doctors had tried a new drug which had worked but left him with some of his right quadriceps gone. He, too, was in his late fifties and retiring soon.

On one of her assignments with him he had told her about the 196 Algorithm in which any set of two or more positive integers is reversed and added to itself. Doing so repetitively yields the result of a palindromic number that reads the same forward and backward. Two examples are: 12 added to 21 is the palindromic number 33; and second; 25 added to 25 is 50, reversed again is 05 added back to 50 yields the palindromic number 55. For larger numbers it takes a little longer to do the addition, but it works.

"Except for 196, it works for every other number, at least out as far as anyone has tried. It's like adding apples and oranges," he said. The problem actually interested her, and that evening, she did some addition to verify the algorithm. She concluded that, if anyone could decipher the number sequence left on the dead woman, Jim could.

"The way the body was mutilated," Ginny observed, "would lead me to believe that either the killer knew her, or it was some sort of a cult ritual. The heart being removed from the chest cavity and a piece of it being bitten off is not something a rapist or thief would do."

"You're right," the captain agreed. "That's why I want you to do a nationwide search to find out if there are any similar murders that are unsolved. If so, we could have a serial killer on our hands."

"I've already done so," she said, smiling. She was a little hurt that he didn't trust her to do that on her own. "Has the bite pattern of the heart been analyzed?" She was assuming that it was a bite pattern.

"Yes," Captain Barr said. "It appears not to have been made by a human. The pattern is too small and the coroner has a preliminary finding of a cat bite. It's also too small for a dog."

"I thought so too. But wouldn't a wild animal have carried the heart away to finish it?"

"Possibly, or it might have been interrupted in the process and didn't think the heart was worth returning for," Captain Clark said. "There weren't any animal tracks on or around the body either, so the bite may have taken place somewhere else. The lack of blood at the scene indicates the woman must have been killed somewhere else and the body placed at that location. You say you've been searching for similarly mutilated bodies already?"

"Yes," she said. "I haven't found anything yet. Either there aren't any or they've been too recent to have been loaded into a database. This could be the first victim too. I'll keep searching and maybe another one will pop up."

"If this is the only one," he said, "it might be a tough case to solve unless the husband did it."

"It would be nearly impossible for the husband to have killed her since he was on a business trip in San Francisco, which has been verified by witnesses. She was also seen alive at a grocery store after he had left."

"Well, keep at it," the captain said. "Something might turn up." He walked back toward his office.

CHAPTER EIGHT

"I can't believe that so many of them have died," Barbara said. She had been the valedictorian of her high school class and the head majorette of the band. She was a very intelligent woman, but because women in the early sixties were expected to get married, raise a family, and stay housewives all their lives, she had never gone further than high school. Not many of her classmates, men or women, had either. Had she been born five years later, she might have been encouraged to go to college. Her parents, like so many that had grown up during the depression and lived through World War II and thought that a woman's place was in the home, didn't have the funds to send a son to college, much less a daughter, and believed children should be on their own as soon as they graduated from high school.

So she got married, had three children, got a divorce, and became a single mom. She tried marriage again, but her second husband was the same as the first when it came to helping around the house. He didn't. That marriage lasted one year and she was alone again raising three children without help. She had not attended every reunion, but she remembered every classmate, if not what they looked like, their names. Considering there were over three hundred, she had to have had an excellent memory. So when she found out how many of her classmates had died, she was appalled. Not only had the number alarmed her, but they were almost all women, and a lot of them had died in the past three years, the first one being Kate Bardydohr.

Barbara was still an attractive woman and had kept her weight down close to what it was in high school. She lived alone in a small cottage behind her son's house and had a white-on-grey merle Great Dane named Charro as her constant companion. She had stayed in the little town in Ohio she had lived in all of her life, did not travel much, and because she did not have any income to spare, did not go out very often. The class reunion was one extravagance she allowed herself in which to participate, and she was on the committee that planned each reunion.

"Yeah," Jeannette said. They had run into each other at the Rite Aid drug and everything-else-you-don't-need store at the prescription counter. "And I think I heard that some of them were murdered." Jeannette had also stayed her entire life in the same small town. She, too, had been married twice (her second marriage lasting) and was on the same reunion committee as Barbara. The joke that had followed Jeannette since high school was that she had only had two dates before she got married, the football team and the band.

"Oh," was all Barbara managed to respond with. Her curiosity was starting to pique and she made a mental note to contact Guido Sarducchi who was the committee member in charge of maintaining the class roster and mailing out all the invitations. He also kept a website containing all the known classmates' information.

"Yes, and they all have died in the last three years," Jeannette said. "We got notices back from their husbands or next of kin when we sent out the first invitations. They were scattered all over the country so it could just be a coincidence, but we aren't old enough to be losing twelve classmates since 1998, all murdered and all women."

"I agree," Barbara said. "Does anyone know anything about how they died?" The clerk, who was listening intently, finished processing her payment and handed her the store's copy of the charge card receipt to sign.

"No. But I mean to ask Guido if he has any more information about them. He has put together a web site and has an "In Memoriam" page with a list of names. Another strange thing about the list is that only a couple of the ones who still lived here have died and they were not murdered. Considering that a lot of the women didn't leave town after graduation, you would think that a higher percentage of dead classmates would be from here, not from out of town."

"You would think so," Barbara said. "Let me know what you find out from Guido. I can also use my computer to search the records of the towns they lived in if he hasn't already done that. I've got to run. Charro has been alone for three hours and probably needs to get out of the house." She picked up the bag her prescription and the copy of the receipt were in and turned to leave while a wide-eyed clerk looked after them.

"See ya at the meeting," Jeannette said.

"That's right, it is this weekend. See ya there," Barbara replied, and headed for her car mulling over what she had just found out.

Two days later, Barbara called Guido and asked about the list. Guido lived in another state, actually several states in the past few years. He rarely answered his phone and used an answering machine most of the time. She felt lucky to catch him instead of having to leave a message.

"Jeannette called me yesterday and asked the same question," Guido said. "I Googled their names last night and

63

came up with three newspaper reports, all from the last year, and they indicated all three were murdered."

"Oh!" she said. "Only three?" She could hear birds in the background and assumed he was outside on a cell phone or cordless home phone.

"That was all I've found so far. Some of the others died more than a year ago, so any of the older stories may be archived. I intend to call the home phone numbers we have for some of the others and do some inquiries. Wanna help?"

"Not yet," she said. She hated to use the phone and only had a cell phone for emergencies. "Let me or Jeannette know what you find out and, if you could, please e-mail me the info you've already found."

"Okay," he said, "but some of the information is not pretty."

"How so?"

"The articles said the bodies had been mutilated, but didn't say how. Two papers used the words 'ritualistically mutilated' without going into details. You'll see what I mean when you read them. I'm bringing copies to the meeting Sunday."

"Okay, thanks," she said and hung up the phone staring blankly at the wall. Charro, who had been lying on the couch next to her, noticed the angst in her voice and muzzled her hand.

"I'm okay, puppy," she said to the dog, scratching him behind the ear. She still called him a puppy even though he was full-grown and outweighed her by forty pounds. "Mama's okay." Charro was not convinced and still had that concerned look in his eyes.

She has a dog, he thought, as he observed from his perch on the hill in the park behind her cottage. He had purposely saved the ones living in his hometown until now. Any suspicious deaths would have caused front-page headlines and sooner or later, someone would notice the similarities. Now he didn't care since his work in the other parts of the country were completed. Only the ones here remained.

Through the 35 mm camera with the 500 mm zoom lens and a 3X magnifier mounted on a tripod, he could read a license plate from a mile or more away. This time, however, he was focused on a couch seen through the living room window less than half a mile distant. He was not using his binoculars as that would look suspicious to the golfers on the adjacent country club course or anyone using the park for their morning walk.

He knew the area well, having played here almost every summer as a young boy who only lived a block from the north entrance to the park. He panned the area from time to time as if searching for some elusive prey to photograph. If anyone asked, he would tell them that he was taking pictures of a red-breasted grosbeak, or some other rare sounding bird. Passersby in the park saw him, golfers saw him, but no one questioned this "photographer."

This will be more difficult, but I know how to handle dogs, he thought as he folded up the tripod, not bothering to remove the camera. Ten minutes later he was gone.

The committee met on the Sunday afternoon four days after Barbara and Jeannette had seen each other in the drugstore. They usually went to a restaurant for dinner and then met afterward at Jeannette's house. This time they were meeting on a Sunday afternoon for lunch, which in this region of the country, was called dinner. Dinner was called supper, which confused visitors until they understood the difference. Their reunion committee meeting would follow over dessert and coffee at Grinders, another dining establishment that allowed them to sit and talk in a quieter atmosphere than the noisy restaurant they were in now. Eight other committee members and their spouses were attending. After one of their members had died suddenly of a heart attack at the age of fifty-eight, the committee chairman had requested that they all meet at least once a month. "…because life is short," he had said. He himself had died of natural causes eighteen months later, but not before naming his successor.

The talk was not about the up-coming fortieth reunion, but about what Barbara and Guido had found out about their female classmates.

"Fifteen have been murdered," Barbara, said. "That can't be a coincidence. "Even though they all live in different states, they all have one thing in common. They were our classmates."

The others were staring at her wide-eyed and mouths agape.

"What scares the hell out of me is that the killer could be one of our classmates," Jeannette said, breaking the silence. "I mean, if they were all killed then who might be next?"

"Get out!" Cassy said. "That scares the hell out of me too." She was the only one who usually came alone to the meetings. She had been divorced twice and that was enough to convince her to become a devout single woman the rest of her life. She lived alone and was, as she thought, more vulnerable than those who might have a man in the house, no matter how much of a bastard he might be.

The other female class members moved a little closer to their husbands as if for protection against a possible predator who could be the man sitting across from them.

"They have more than being our classmates in common," Barbara said. Here are copies of the newspaper reports we downloaded from the internet." She passed the stapled pages to Angela, who was seated on her right. Not waiting for the papers to be passed to them, the other women got up and crowded around Angela's chair.

"Ritual killings?" Angela asked. "What do they mean ritual killings?"

"There was one article which mentioned that the victim's

heart had been removed from her chest cavity," Barbara said. This was not news that Mavis, the most squeamish of the group, wanted to hear. She turned ashen and slumped back in her chair next to Angela.

The others put their hands to their mouths as if to keep from tossing their lunch. A lunch they hadn't even ordered yet and might not after they read the reports. Certainly their appetites would be somewhat curbed.

As he neared the cottage, the dog barked. It was a deep throated bark, one that would certainly warn and scare off any other intruder but him. He had an ample supply of jerky in his pocket which would calm any dog. Food was dogs' language and anyone who fed them, they seemed to think, could not be all that bad. He planned on making several trips to visit the dog when no one was home, so the dog would remain calm in his presence as he waited in the cottage for its owner to return.

He tried the door and found it to be unlocked. *That's a pleasant surprise*, he thought. The Great Dane had quit barking and was eyeing him through the door window which started halfway up the door. His tail was wagging which indicated he was friendly and probably would not hurt him if he didn't threaten the dog. The dog was also wearing a collar with a tag which was big enough to be read.

"Charro!" he called softly to the dog. It was not the same as the sexy dancer, Charo, which was spelled with one "r", but he recognized it as the Spanish word for "corrupt." It was also the name of an Elvis Presley movie, one of his least noteworthy and one in which the only song he had sung was the theme song of the same name. Neither the song nor the movie made it to the charts. He remembered that Barbara's mother had been a huge Elvis fan, huge, with capital letters. Barbara's mother, he remembered, was attractive and friendly. Barbara's father, on the other hand, was protective and like most fathers in the fifties was a grouch.

The dog seemed startled to hear his name coming from a stranger, but only stopped wagging for a second. He pulled out a piece of jerky, opened the door a crack, and offered the meat to the dog. The dog took one whiff and quickly grabbed the jerky as if it would not be offered much longer. Charro backed off and he opened the door. The dog sat back on its haunches and raised its right paw as if in a handshake. He shook the offered paw and quickly gave him another piece of jerky.

"Good boy," he said, noticing that Charro had a penis but his sack was the thickness of a quarter. "Oh, they had ya fixed, huh boy?" The dog stuck its massive head in the direction of another piece of jerky. "That's what all the women want to do to men," he added.

"Here ya go. I've got a lot more for ya, boy. Good dog." He came in and sat down on the sofa that was covered with a blanket and canvas protector. This was where the dog must have spent most of his time while his mistress was away. The dog seemed to like the attention and was obviously a "people" dog. It must be quite lonely in the cottage where he couldn't even see passersby on the sidewalk. The cottage was at least 150 feet behind the main house which was another 100 feet from the street.

The dog immediately jumped up onto the couch and lay down with its head and large paws across his lap. He stroked the dog for a long time while he watched the TV which was on, probably to entertain the dog. It was the HG TV cable channel, and the dog probably just liked the noise it provided. He didn't know how much time he would have so decided to leave after fifteen minutes.

He looked around the cottage. He was sitting on the couch in the living room, a room full of items which looked like the remnants of many a garage sale. There was only an eight-by-ten-foot section in the middle of the floor that did not have anything on it except a rug with dog toys and a pile of well-chewed bones. On the small table in the far left corner of the room was a stack of crossword puzzles, some anagrams, and sudokus all neatly completed. *So, she likes to do puzzles*, he thought. *I'll give her some puzzles to work on.*

"Not much room to move around in here is there?" he said aloud. The dog lifted its head as if in acknowledgement, put its head back down, and let out a snort of agreement. He noticed for the first time that the red collar around the dog was a shock collar used with invisible fences. Looking toward the door, he saw the two red lights of the transmitter box attached to the wall under a set of light switches.

"Well at least you have enough room outside to run around in," he said. The dog did not respond to this statement. He sat there through the rest of the TV program in which a kid's room was being transformed into something he considered hideous. *The kid will outgrow the room in three or four years*, he thought. *Then what?*

"I gotta get up, boy," he said. When he did, the dog looked disappointed. He surveyed the rest of the cottage, which consisted of two bedrooms, one turned into a combination library, computer room, and dog pen and another looked hardly used except for storage. There was a small bathroom and kitchen which were adequate for one person. All were decorated with the paraphernalia similar to that found in the living room. The dog followed him around as if tethered to his hip.

On his second trip to the computer room, he found some interesting papers laid out on top of the printer.

"What have we here?" he said, picking up the papers. Charro put his nose on the papers he was examining. "Looks like they're curious about their murdered classmates and have copies of some of the newspaper articles. I'd better do some more snooping."

He sat down on an old wooden office chair and moved the mouse to wake up the laptop computer sitting on the desk in front of him, interrupting the screen saver consisting of a parade of personal photos. "Lookie here," he said to the dog.

Charro stuck his massive nose on top of his new-best-friend's right arm as if he were reading the computer screen. The dog left a wet mark on the top of his forearm when he retreated a moment later. He clicked on the Wal-Mart symbol which connected the modem to the internet service provider. The log-in screen popped up a second later with the woman's name as the user and asterisks filling in the password section. He clicked on the "logon" button and he could hear the dialer doing its job.

After a couple of minutes, the computer sounded "welcome," followed by "you've got mail!" The dog retreated to a canvas bed on the side of the room closest to the porch he had come in from. He commenced gnawing on a bone that was stashed beside the bed.

"Well, well," he said, as he opened the mail inbox. There were some older messages which had attachments containing the articles he had found on the printer. He took a pencil from the top shelf of the desk and tore off a Post-it-note from the pad next to the pencil. He jotted down the sender's e-mail address and information from the various other messages in the in-box and saved folders. He also opened the address book and wrote some of that information down too. He e-mailed the information to himself and then deleted the copy of the message just sent from the sent folder and then from the deleted folder. *I'll have some fun with this*, he thought.

"Charro," he said, getting the dog's immediate attention. "I've gotta go. Maybe I can stay a little longer next time." As he got up, the dog got up too and followed him into the living room. When he reached for the door knob, the dog started to whine, obviously sad to see his new-found friend leaving him. "Here," he said, and reached in his pocket for another piece of jerky. He tossed it toward the center of the floor and as the dog turned to retrieve it, he opened the door and left. The dog barked a couple of times as if saying goodbye and then was silent. He walked back into the woods and headed for his truck that he had left at the park less than a half a mile away.

That evening from my hotel room I sent her some e-mails, all made to look like they had come from her friend Guido who had sent her the newspaper articles. Attached to the emails were all the number codes I had used so far, and one I hadn't used – yet.

31	21	21	14	0
31	20	20	31	0
31	20	22	13	0
31	21	21	14	0
31	0	0	0	0
0	4	4	4	0
31	1	1	1	0
31	17	17	31	0
31	1	1	31	0
0	0	0	0	0
16	8	7	8	16
31	17	17	31	0
31	1	1	31	0
0	0	24	0	0
31	20	22	13	0
31	21	21	17	0
0	0	0	0	0
31	8	4	2	31
31	21	21	17	0
16	10	4	10	16
16	16	31	16	16

If she and her friends were able to decode this set of numbers, they would find out who was next on the list.

Chapter Nine

Barbara was sitting at the small desk where she kept her notebook computer. She had just printed out the coded messages which she believed Guido had sent her. They were spread out in front of her in no particular order.

I wonder how he got these? She thought. She jerked up a bit when her concentration was broken by footsteps on the front porch and the immediate barking of Charro. The window that would allow her to look out onto the porch was behind her and to the left so she missed seeing whoever was there. The dog, however, did not. He was immediately off the couch, his large head peering out the top half of the front door. He had stopped barking and was wagging his tail indicating it was someone he was familiar with.

The dog liked to see another person, tired of playing by himself or with the cats all day, that is, when the cats allowed him to torment them. Some of his torments got him a scratch on the nose, but that was part of the game to Charro. He had lots of nose to scratch. The cats in turn would bring him part of their "catch" du jour, usually a mouse or squirrel which they unceremoniously placed on the rug outside the door, much to the delight of Charro. Barbara then had the dubious pleasure of taking the carcass away from the dog who was tossing it, shaking it, and running around the yard, part of his game of owners keepers.

"GB! (short for Grandma Barbi)," came the shout from David, who was waiting on the other side of the door. He had stopped short of opening the door and walking in, waiting so that his grandmother, could hold back Charro. The dog would attack him as soon as David came through the door. It was not malice on Charro's part, merely a greeting, but the dog outweighed David by eighty pounds and could knock him down just with the dog's enthusiasm. Barbara rose and slowly walked around the dividing wall between her library and the living room. She didn't like being interrupted, but she had agreed to watch David between the time he got home from school and when his mother or father, Barbara's son, arrived home from work.

"Wait until I get him a bone," she said. She went to the refrigerator and as soon as she opened the freezer, Charro immediately pulled away from the entering David and ran to the kitchen, about four steps for the animal. She handed the dog a large soup bone, still frozen, which he immediately grabbed and retreated to the living room to gnaw on, forgetting completely about the arrival of the nine-year old boy. She got the bones from a country butcher shop near where one of her daughters lived (the older daughter). She boiled the bones, and gave the dog one almost every night to keep him busy while she ate her own dinner.

"What are you doing?" David asked. He almost never used slang words or contractions and spoke each syllable of every word succinctly. He was what is called a "late talker" and still had a bit of a lisp which he would hopefully outgrow, but not before being teased by his classmates. His uncle, Barbara's brother, once asked what was wrong with the kid, after

73

David had answered his uncle's phone call question 'where's your father?' very politely with 'I do not know,' instead of the expected 'I dunno.' David was also very bright, especially in math and the sciences. He obviously had inherited some of his intelligence from Barbara's side of the family. He most likely would become the first male and only the third child in the lineage to go to college.

"I'm working on my computer," she said.

"What are you doing on the computer?" he asked. Having grown up in the computer age, David, like so many other kids his age, was computer literate.

"Searching for something," she said heading back to the computer with David close behind. Charro watched them for a second and then went back to crunching on his bone. As Barbara sat down, David noticed the coded messages.

"What are these?" he asked, picking up one of the sheets acting like the dog with his nose in the open refrigerator.

"They're some sort of code," she responded, acting a bit irritated, but accepting his actions as part of being the grandmother of a curious and questioning child.

"May I see them?" he asked, grabbing another one of the sheets without waiting for an answer.

David had to rely on his own resources for entertainment. He lived on a street where there were no other kids to play with. Unlike in the fifties when his grandmother was his age, today's children did not play in the neighborhood or, for that matter, their own front yards. Even this small town of less than thirty thousand had its share of sexual predators. His sister was six years younger than he, so except for rare occasions when he had a school friend for a sleepover, he had to search for something to do on his own. In the summer, when not at baseball practice or playing in a game, David "helped" his grandmother putter in the yard.

In the "big house," he had a game console connected to the TV, but in the cottage, his fun had to come by other means. Sometimes his grandmother let him use her computer, but it had dial up and was very slow compared to his own connection to the high-speed modem his mother used. Unlike his father who shunned all forms of electronic devices except his company-provided cell phone and the TV remote control, David was technically proficient.

David studied the code he had picked up while GB continued her quest on eBay for a new glass cabinet door and cabinet hinges. She was remodeling the kitchen after one of her favorite programs on the H&G cable TV program.

"It looks like digitally coded binary," David said, turning the page on its side.

"Wha', what?" Barbara said, irritated that her concentration had been broken once again. She looked at the piece of paper and turned her facial expression into a fist by tightening all her facial muscles at once. "What are you talking about?"

"I have a clock that shows the time in binary and sometimes the lights on its face look like letters." He picked up a pencil and drew arranged dots on the page in the shape of the capital letter T. Five dots formed the top of the letter. Then he started to write down the binary equivalent for the letter T.

"See, the first dot on the left, at the top of the T is binary sixteen. The one next to it and all the others, except the middle dots, are also sixteen. The middle column of dots is sixteen plus eight, plus four, plus two, plus one. That's thirty one." Her look now was one of surprise with her eyebrows raised.

"See," he continued, pointing to numbers on the page, "this row of numbers sixteen, sixteen, thirty-one, sixteen, and sixteen are the letter T." He looked up now to see GB with her mind racing over the rest of the coded data.

"Go get me that clock," she said.

Charro looked up from his bone long enough to see the boy racing through the living room, grabbing his jacket on the way out, enthusiastic to be able to help his grandmother.

"I will be right back," he said politely as he slammed the door. While he was gone, GB picked up the coded messages, marking each one that met the criteria with the letter T.

When he returned at a run with the clock, she had finished filling in the Ts. There were at least a dozen of them. David found an empty outlet on the power strip at the side of the desk and plugged in the clock. He took a moment to catch his breath while she studied the blinking LED lights.

"David, this clock doesn't look like what you described," she said. "It doesn't have five lights in each column. The first one only has two, the third and fifth only three, and the others only four." She pointed to each column of red LEDs as she said this.

"I know, GB," he said. She didn't really care for the initialized version of Grandma Barbi, especially when he was the only one who did it and he usually pronounced each syllable as if it were a forbidden letter. He had picked up the acronym from one of her old boyfriends who had used the term around her grandchildren. David was excited to be able to help out and do something other than watch TV. In addition to being a little out of breath, he was speaking excitedly and taking shortcuts with his speech.

"This is a binary clock and doesn't need all the lights to have four columns," he continued. "See, the first column goes up to two and then starts over." He held down the hour set button in the back of the clock so that it would go quickly through the time change.

"Why two?" she interrupted.

"It can be a twenty-four hour clock," he said, and then continued. "See, the second column only has to go up to nine before it resets which is the top dot representing eight and the bottom dot representing one." He was referring to the lights as dots, which is what they appeared to be from a distance when the clock was turned on. "The third column only has to go up to six, which is the top dot representing four, and the next dot representing two. Those dots added together are six." She looked at him with a "duh" look, wanting to tell him that she knew how to add, but held her tongue.

"The last two rows are the seconds," he concluded, looking at her with his deep brown eyes sparkling. "When I am in my room, I sometimes watch the clock spell out letters. At seven twenty seven and seven seconds it has the letter "H" and the letter "I" spelling out "HI." That's the only word I have noticed so far. Here, let me show you." He did the fast forward until the clock was seven twenty seven and then let it run the seven seconds, holding it so she could see.

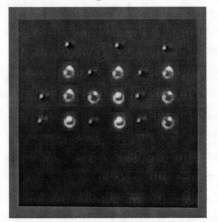

"That's interesting," she said.

He continued, ignoring her interruption. "The others I have noticed are just letters like little "o" on the twenty-four hour clock at seven minutes and fifty seven seconds after midnight."

"What are you doing up at midnight?" she wondered, saying it out loud.

"Only in the summer," he came back with quickly. She let it rest. "See, if there are four lights in each column and it went to the highest numbers before resetting, the clock would spell out a lot of letters."

"Yes," she said. "And if there were a lot of these columns

with five lights high, they would spell out words and sentences." She was visualizing the several columns of dots like the old piano rolls used by the first automated pianos. She also recalled the punch cards the very first computers used for entering data, only those were rectangular holes.

"How did you learn this?" she asked.

"Mr. Andreazzi at school," he said. She could have guessed this. She had met the teacher at the grandparent's day event at the school and he had struck her as very progressive and innovative in his approach to teaching.

"He taught us that computers count in binary numbers," he said.

"Binary numbers?" she asked. Her mind was going a mile a minute trying to decode the messages in front of her, but didn't want to discourage David, who was very excited to be able to discuss something he was interested in.

"Yes," he went on. "The binary scale is like our decimal scale but the scale only goes to two and then the base is exceeded and you have to start over. It's just like our counting system that goes to nine and the next count exceeds the base and we start over with a one and a zero. There are ten numbers, zero being a number. Mr. Andreazzi said that because all computers do is add ones and zeros, they are not very smart machines, but they add very quickly."

As David finished this last statement, the phone rang. Barbara ordinarily cringed when she had to answer a call, but this time she welcomed the interruption because it put David on hold. He might have gone on for a long time.

It was David's mom and she had his dinner ready. She made him french-fries, one of only two or three foods David ate. He had had an allergy to some food as a baby and through experimentation, they found what did not make him sick. He had not gotten used to any other food and therefore did not like anything but what his mom prepared for him. David had sensed that it was his mom calling him home and was headed to the bedroom to retrieve his coat.

"Tell her I'm on my way!" he cried out as he turned the corner into the bedroom.

She did so and then picked up a pencil to decipher the messages. She started with the one on top, the message about her.

Chapter Ten

"Who called this meeting?" Bill asked. He said the same thing at the beginning of every meeting and got the same answer, no response. There was a good turnout for this meeting in spite of the damp weather.

The meeting was taking place in the garage at Jeannette and Rob's house on the north end of town. Everyone had brought a small dish and Rob was grilling chicken breasts as the main entrée. Until the discovery of murdered classmates replaced it, food seemed to have been the bond that kept the group together.

Barbara was animated as she handed out copies of the translated messages. No one could recall her having this much enthusiasm for anything. Even in high school, despite being the head majorette, she was always laid back. Nothing was a challenge to her, so she had let her mind wander in class way back then. The only non-A grade she had ever received was an F for not doing an assignment she felt was silly. Her other grades in the class were so high, the failing grade had had no effect on the final outcome.

"What is this stuff?" Jeannette asked, leafing hurriedly through the twenty pages of coded messages Barbara had handed to her. As soon as she had seen enough of each sheet, Jeannette passed them one at a time to Cassy, sitting to her right.

"Guido sent them to me," Barbara said, "Only when I e-mailed him to ask where he had gotten them, he didn't know what I was talking about. I forwarded one of the e-mails with the coded message back to him and he said he had never seen them before. They were sent to me using his e-mail address, so I don't know what the hell is going on." They all looked at her in disbelief, partly because they had never heard her use a swear word, and partly because they wondered what this revelation meant.

Pablo, who had spent a lot of time with sailors working on a cruise ship, had once said that Barbara wouldn't say "shit" if she had a mouth full of it. He looked up from his can of beer with his mouth open. Cassy's only comment to Pablo's mouth-full-of-shit comment had been "EEEWW!"

"This one says 'Barbi-Lou you're next.'" Cassy read aloud.

"I know," Barbara responded. "It's translated just as I've indicated, with the dash and the apostrophe. The key to the code I used must be right to pull all that out of it."

"Some of these are nasty," Darleen said, as she picked up the one Cassy had just passed to her. "Look at this one! 'The bitch deserved it.' And this one, 'blondes eat shit.'" The police report (not released to the public) stated in part, "Fecal matter, source not yet determined, was found in victim's mouth and throat, presumably inserted after death."

"If you're next," Lucy said, after seeing the one addressed to Barbi-Lou, "you better get police protection." Lucy worked as a reporter on the local paper and knew almost every important official in town. "I can talk to Chief Dorian if you want. The chief of police is running for sheriff next year and could use some positive publicity. If this information helps solve a case, then he would be better known throughout the county. He would also know who to contact at a national level about all this."

"It's gotta be someone you know," Angela said. "He used your nickname instead of your real name."

"He could have gotten that from your personalized license plate," Mavis observed. Mavis had known Barbara since grade school. Most of the others in the committee had gone to the schools at the north end of town, but Mavis and Barbara, with the exception of kindergarten through third grade, attended elementary and junior high together on the south end.

"The spelling on my license plate does not have an "o" in the middle of Lou," Barbara said. "It must have been someone who heard me called Barbi-Lu, but didn't know how I spelled it."

"That could be important," Angela said.

"You guys are scaring the hell out of me," Jeannette said.

"Can you get me copies of these," Lucy asked. "I'll give them to the chief and see what he says."

"You can have those," Barbara said. "I have the originals on my computer back at my place."

"Who came up with the code translations?" Bill asked.

"My grandson," Barbara said. "He guessed what the numbers meant the first time he saw them."

"Damn Nintendo generation knows everything," Bill added.

With the meeting ended, everyone set out on their assignments, and with next month's meeting scheduled, they all said their goodbyes and some hugged. Not only did they plan events, they enjoyed each other's company and looked forward to the monthly meetings.

Lucy took the codes and translations to discuss the

situation with Chief Dorian as soon as she could get an appointment to meet with him. Barbara was anxious to get home as she didn't want to leave Charro alone for too long, especially during daylight hours. She knew he would sleep most of the time, but he would miss his afternoon walk.

He and Charro were getting to be best friends. This was the third time he had visited the little cottage and brought the dog treats. Parking his truck on a side street not far from the front of the main house in front of the cottage, he had walked across the street and through the parking lot of the local country club. There was no activity today since just enough of a light mist was falling to keep the golfers off the course.

At the south end of the parking lot was a wooded area. The trees, black walnut, oak, maple, and hickory covered the steep hill that formed the back side of all the properties abutting the fairways from the parking lot to the park from where he had first observed the cottage. The trees served as a buffer for the noise of cursing golfers and also deflected the stray golf balls back onto the course. Not all of them, but enough to keep hooked and sliced balls from breaking any windows in the cottage.

As a child, he and his friends would comb the woods for stray balls and sell them back to the golfers to use on the driving range. They also lay low in the woods by the first hole which was concealed from the tee by a bend and a slight uphill grade. A large school bell by the first hole was rung by departing golfers when the green was cleared, thus alerting the next group that it was safe to tee off. When a ball ventured too close to the woods, the boys would dart out and swipe the ball retreating to the safety of the woods. If spotted they would run back deeper into the woods and into the adjoining park. No one followed them, but to be on the safe side, whenever they were discovered, they stopped their ball snatching for a few days until they thought it would be safe again.

So it was easy for him to walk through the trees to the back of the cottage three lots away. There was a path indicating that someone had been using the woods as a hiking trail and there were no shrubs to block his way.

No wonder there was a trail, he thought. *This was an enjoyable way to get some exercise.*

It was probably used by one of the adults who lived adjacent to the golf course. Kids did not play outside anymore unless an adult organized some sort sport like baseball, football, or soccer. Back when he was a young boy, the neighborhood kids organized their own sports and had a lot of fun doing it. If they wanted to go out of their own neighborhood, they hopped on their Schwinns and Huffys and pedaled there.

When he got to the back of the cottage, Charro immediately started his deep barking. As soon as the dog looked through the screen door and saw him standing on the porch, the barking stopped and he started wagging his tail. He wagged so hard his whole rear end moved. It was amazing how the dog respected the screen door because at well over one hundred pounds, he could easily have pushed it open.

He had the usual treat for the dog, chicken jerky, which the dog seemed to love as much as David loved french fries. When he got inside, he noticed the place had been rearranged since his last visit. After giving the dog some much demanded attention in addition to the jerky, he walked to the adjacent room to use the computer. He suspected that she may have changed her e-mail server since, as of a couple of days ago, he could no longer access her e-mail. Getting into her computer would enable him to find her new e-mail address.

Noticing that the computer room was rearranged too, he immediately saw why he could not get into her e-mail anymore. She now had a DSL modem and a new computer. Gone was the laptop. *She finally got off that god-awful dial-up,* he thought. When he sat down at the computer desk, Charro, as if on cue, lay down beside him on the floor. It seemed the dog knew that this was not the time to ask for more treats.

Just as he had accomplished what he was there for, the dog growled, started barking and ran to the door. Glancing over to the window overlooking the porch, he saw someone pass by.

Damn, can't be her, the person was too short, he thought. As he heard the screen door open, he ducked into the bathroom across from the computer room. In the commotion of the dog jumping around as he greeted whoever was at the door, he was able to pull the shower curtain to the bathtub shut undetected. He moved against the back wall of the tub and remained perfectly still.

"Stop, Charro! Stop!" the young boy in the living room shouted. The dog must have settled down as the boy was now talking softly to him. He heard the boy go into the kitchen, open the refrigerator and close it again. He then heard the distinctive pop of a can being opened. As the footsteps passed in front of the bathroom door, he heard the interloper belch.

Nice manners, he thought. *But then kids see that on TV all the time now, along with farting, and think nothing of it.* The movie, *Shrek,* was a fine example where, in the opening scene, the main character farts in a pond and picks up the fish that float to the surface, overcome by gaseous fumes. Even he had laughed at that, but that sort of behavior was never done in public when he was a boy. The cowboys in the movies he went to see as a kid didn't belch and fart, not even the bad ones wearing black hats.

He remained as still as he could. He could hear the kid playing video games, probably over the internet. His own computer must have been broken, and seeing that his grandmother was not at home, he decided to use hers. Just as fatigue was setting in and his legs were getting tired of standing, he heard the chair scoot back and the kid walk in his direction. The kid unzipped his pants and lifted the lid to the toilet up not more than three feet away from his hiding place in the tub.

He heard him pissing and then the lid dropped with a loud bang. He nearly jumped out of his shoes, but still managed not to make a sound.

As the kid started back out of the bathroom, the shower curtain started to poke through in the middle. *That damn dog is trying to get behind the curtain*, he thought. *He must know I'm in here.* The dog then started to whine and half yelp as if coaxing him out from behind the curtain.

"Charro!" the boy said. "Quiet. Please, shut up!" Then he heard the boy approaching. He had never harmed a child and if he did now, the dog was surely going to take sides and he would have to do something about Charro too. Maybe if he just scared both of them, he might be able to get away. His plans for Barbi-lou might then be spoiled. Luckily, the boy just wanted to get Charro to stop whining.

"Come on, Charro," he said, but the dog did not leave. "Look what I have."

The boy must have gotten the dog a treat from one of the shelves in the library. He had noticed the treats before, a large assortment of bones, rawhide, Pupperoni, and tooth cleaning snacks.

There was a bit of a struggle of some sort, probably the dog trying to turn around as quickly as possible in the tiny bathroom. Then the pocket door to the bathroom slid shut. *Thank God*, he thought. *Now, if the boy will only leave before she gets back, I'm out of here and back in business.*

But the boy apparently had no intentions of leaving. He was on the computer and making sounds as if he were playing a game. The new computer had come with a nineteen-inch, LCD monitor with built-in speakers, just right for gaming.

No leaving now, he thought, since the computer desk was just across from the bathroom door. Any movement on his part was sure to arouse the dog, so he sat down in the tub with his back against the side opposite the spigots. About five minutes later he fell asleep.

He had had the dream before, one of being pursued down a long dark alley with no way out. This time, instead of the pursuer being a cat, it was a dog. As the dog trapped him in a corner behind a dumpster, teeth snarling and eyes blazing red, he jolted awake.

Something had stirred Charro and the dog started barking.

Was I thrashing around in the tub? He thought. *Was I snoring?* It turned out to be neither. The dog had gone into the other room and was barking at something outside the bedroom window.

"Oh, oh!" David said. "Grandma Barbi must be home." There was some movement at the computer as the dog thundered by the bathroom door heading toward the front door, the only way in or out.

Shit, he thought. *What'll I do now?* He stood up at the ready in case he was discovered. He had no weapons, but the surprise of finding someone in your bathroom might allow him just enough time to push his way out. But, only if the dog and the boy didn't get in the way. There was also the possibility she might recognize him after forty years, but maybe not in the commotion.

"Hi GB," the boy said as the door to the cottage opened.

"Puppy sitting?" she asked.

"Yes," he lied. "I came down to see if Charro needed to go out."

"Oh," she said. "Did he?" Then added, "Why is the bathroom door shut?"

"Charro was in there making a lot of noise and I couldn't get him to come out."

"Did he go outside at all?" she asked.

"No, he did not."

"How long have you been down here?"

"Not long," he lied again.

"Well," she said. "I'm going to take Charro for a walk."

Great! he thought, from his hiding place in the tub. *Then I can leave.*

"Sure," the boy said. "I'll get his leash and go with you."

"First I need to use the bathroom," she said.

Damn it! He thought. He got back against the far wall of the bathtub and got ready to spring out if necessary. The shower curtain was opaque and it also had a dark liner. Not much light came in, and if he stayed perfectly still, she would not know he was there.

He heard footsteps softly approaching, the pocket door slide open, and then the door slide shut again. She lifted the lid to the toilet and sat down. The noise of her urinating almost made him snicker. He wondered if he could make her shit by jumping out from behind the curtain.

After a few seconds, he could hear her grab some toilet paper and the soft sound of wiping. She stood up and, as David had done, accidentally dropped the lid making him jump, but still he made no noise. She jiggled the handle before she flushed and then he heard the sound of water running. One of the faucets on the sink made a squealing sound as if the washer needed replaced. She then dried her hands on the towel next to the tub, jostling the shower curtain just a little.

"Down, Charro, down," he heard from the other room. The boy must be trying to put the leash on the dog.

"I'm ready," she said, as she slid the pocket door open and exited the bathroom without closing the door. Charro would not be interested in him this time as he was anxious to go for a walk.

As he heard their footsteps leaving the porch, he exited the bathroom. As the dog had done, he went to the bedroom window to make sure the coast was clear. While he was watching, the trio stopped to open the gate. Charro turned around and noticed him looking at them. He let out a little bark, but turned back around and went with them down the driveway.

Convinced no one else was around, he left, walking back the same way he had come, through the path in the woods, to the parking lot, and then to his truck in the street. He got in his truck and headed back out of town passing the three dog walkers on the sidewalk a half block away. Charro stopped and turned toward the truck, looking at him one last time.

CHAPTER 11

"How's our code-buster doing," Chief Barr asked.

"I still don't see any correlation among the numbers," Detective Jim responded. "All the substitutions of letters for numbers don't make sense. It must be some random code, or it morphs as it goes.

"Maybe it's the same thing each time, only different," Jim continued, spitting out one of his malapropisms.

Those who had been around Jim for some time had heard so many of his sayings that they were ignored. Anyone who was new to the office would stare and try to figure out if he intended the statement or if that was just the way his mind worked.

One of the men who worked with Jim swore that his sayings were unintentional, a result of smoking too much pot during the Vietnam War. Jim had been a good detective and as retirement day rapidly approached this would most likely be his last case. He had recently quit smoking, something his newly acquired wife had coerced him into doing. As a consequence he had added a little weight to his six-foot-one frame. Several times a minute he unconsciously tugged at his graying mustache as a substitute for putting a cigarette in his mouth. He talked about 'making money head over heels' as a private investigator as soon as he retired.

"You have to do something when you retire," he would say. "It's either sink or tread water."

"I've tried several ideas, but discarded them as making no sense," he added.

"Well, just be careful you don't forget to dot your T's and cross your I's, or visa versa," Chief Barr said, adding a malapropism of his own and then walking away.

"Where did you get these?" Chief Dorian asked.

"From one of my high school classmates," Lucy said, and gave him Barbara's name. "She said she found one of them in her house and got the others from a classmate through some e-mails. Only the classmate said he had never sent them to her."

"I need to talk to her," Chief said. "She received them with the codes written down?"

"No, her grandson was able to decode them." The chief glanced at her with a disbelieving look and then shook his head.

"Humph," he said. "Ain't that sumpthin'? I mean, look at these!"

LIFE AS A BITCH AND THEN SHE DIES
THE BITCH DESERVED IT
NO PIECE SO SHE GOT PEACE
PUT HER OUT FOR NO PUT OUT
NICE NOSE BUT NO HOSE
WHEN IN DOUBT SNUFF HER OUT
TRY AND FIND ME
BLONDS EAT SHIT
BARBI-LOU YOU'RE NEXT

"The last one," Lucy told him, "refers to Barbara, who received the coded copies. We think the rest refer to the other classmates, all women, who were brutally murdered. Because of my connections with other newspapers and reporters, I was able to obtain copies of police reports of most of the murders." She took the chronologically organized reports out of her still open briefcase and gave them to him.

"We suspect one of our classmates is behind this," she said, and as soon as she had said it she knew what he would be asking next and felt stupid for not bringing him the roster.

"Do you have a list of all the classmates?" he asked.

"Yes, the ones who graduated with us." she said.

"Just from your graduating class?"

"That's what seems to be the connection to all of them," she continued. "We have the names and last known addresses of all our classmates along with some who didn't graduate with us but were in our AHS graduating class at least one of the years we were there. There were two new local high schools that opened for students during our sophomore and junior years. Some transferred and graduated at the new schools. The rest were either held back or dropped out. Even with the transfers, we had over three hundred in our graduating class. I didn't bring a copy of the list, but here is the website that has the latest copy." She wrote down the site address on one of her business cards.

"Your class has a website?" the chief asked.

"Yes. One of our classmates developed it for our upcoming reunion and for the benefit of those who can't attend."

"Any names come to mind of someone who could have held a grudge after all these years?" he asked.

"We asked ourselves that question at our last meeting, and I've gone over the names a dozen times, but no one stands out," Lucy replied. "There were several cliquish groups, but no one felt threatened then or has since."

"What about a woman who might be doing this?" Chief asked. "You know. One who might have been jealous of someone stealing a boyfriend?"

"I don't know," she said. "The murders were brutal and I don't know if a woman would be capable of cutting someone's heart out. We're talking at least fifteen women and there were no guys in our class that good looking."

"Oh there are some women who have done violent murders," Chief said. "Lizzie Borden for one, and then there is Elizabeth Bathory who used cats to help her kill women and then bathed in the victims' blood. The Bathory case comes to mind since one of these reports mentions small animal bites to the removed heart." He held up the first report that was on the stack.

"Okay. I'll download the class roster from the website, and tell Barbara that I'll be calling her. In the meantime, I'll find out if someone in any other state is heading up an investigation and I'll get in contact with them. Then we'll go from there," he concluded. He stood up and walked from behind his desk, a gesture indicating their meeting was done. Lucy got up and headed toward the door as the chief was reaching for the doorknob.

"Thanks," he said as she left. He was already assessing the impact of any breakthroughs he could develop in this case. Breakthroughs would give him some great publicity with the local *Review* and other county newspapers. He was planning on retiring next year and running for county sheriff. *Hell*, he thought. *This could go state and national!*

"Some hick that claims he's the Piece of Chalief in Alliance is on the phone," Jim said, holding up the phone with one hand over the mouthpiece and offering it to Ginny Joynt. In addition to his malapropisms, Jim liked to mispronounce words, sometimes on purpose, sometimes unknowingly.

"Where the hell is Alliance?" he asked furrowing his

brow.

"Northeast of here," Ginny said. "It's near Canton. You've heard of the Mount Union Purple Raiders?"

"Yep," Jim replied. "That's the football team that almost never loses and scores big against their opponents."

"The same," she said, taking the phone from Jim. "Mount Union College is in Alliance."

Jim went back to his desk and sat down, but still listened to one side of the conversation. It sounded as if someone else had information about the case they were working on. Ginny's eyes were wide with excitement the entire time she was talking to the chief from Alliance. Jim pretended not to be interested, but could barely contain his curiosity.

Hanging up the phone she said to Jim, "Wanna go for a ride?"

"Where to?" he asked, acting as if he were not that interested. But he was, terribly so. This was a serial killer case, he was sure of it. Nothing excited him more than being able to use all the skills he had learned over his twenty years as a patrolman and another twenty as a detective. This was different from investigating black-on-black homicides in Columbus' near east side in and around the Driving Park area.

Driving Park received its name from its historic past as a large racing complex for horses and eventually automobiles during the 19th century and early 20th century. Columbus residents would travel to Driving Park to enjoy the exciting horse races held there. When automobiles came to fruition during the 1900s, the track was converted to allow for auto racing. Its largely flat, stretched-oval design allowed turn of the century speedsters to set many records at the track. One major event was the world's first twenty-four-hour race in 1905. The resulting community of Driving Park was small and consisted of employees of the racetrack. During the 1930s, the racetrack was abandoned, yet the community continued to grow and now it is almost all impoverished, uneducated blacks. Poverty begets crime, and Driving Park had its share of murders.

"Alliance," she said when he had asked where. "I want to talk to the chief in Alliance today so if we leave this morning, we can get back late tonight and not have to stay overnight. The chief in Alliance has talked to a person who may have some info on this heart-eating killer. I'll go clear it with Chief Barr, but I'm sure he'll okay it."

"I'm ready," Jim said, getting up from his desk. "I'll go check out a vehicle."

I changed my mind about Barbara being next and decided on Janet. Janet lived near Columbus, and the address was on Golf Village Drive, a golfing community northwest of Columbus. This would have to be a quick and dirty job since most people in the community probably knew everybody else who lived there. I wouldn't be able to park my car close by or find an easy observation point.

For this job I would use my bicycle to get into the neighborhood. On other bike rides I had taken the cat, Dedra, with me. I had sewn some pockets on the backs of some of my bike jackets where the cat could rest her hind legs while stretching out over my shoulder and holding on with her front paws. I had also sewn some padding on the front part of the jersey where Dedra could dig in with her front claws and keep her balance. On previous bike rides with her, I had attracted a lot of attention as the two of us glided along a bike path. It was for that reason that she was not coming with me on this trip. To someone seeing a lone biker I would not be noteworthy, but with a cat on my shoulders I was sure to be remembered.

Wearing a helmet and nondescript jersey, I was able to ride by the house without much notice. Some of the neighbors waved to me as I pedaled by. I waved back but never looked at them directly. Even if I had looked in their direction, with a helmet and tinted goggles, I would be hard to identify. There was a grove of trees across the road to the northwest and from there I would have an unobstructed view of the front of her house. My bike was a hybrid, which meant it was suitable for some off-road riding. As I rode back to the main road, I came upon a golf cart path and took a little detour using it.

I was in luck. The cart lane snaked through the backyards of another portion of the golfing community, but I saw no one. About a quarter mile to the southeast, I crossed a road, then ducked under some trees and out to one end of a green. The golf path took me east and then south on what looked like the other side of the woods that I wanted access to. A glance at the bike's GPS confirmed this. I was about two hundred yards away and to the west. There were no golfers in view so I ducked into the woods with my bike. The trees were dense enough to prohibit undergrowth from hampering my pedaling.

According to my GPS, I was heading due east. Halfway into the woods, I was completely obscured from the golf green. A little further and I could see her house peeking out from behind the tree trunks. I spotted a tall oak tree with a limb close to the ground which would offer me a perch for viewing unnoticed. I doubted anyone would follow me into the woods, but if they did, I could hear well enough to detect them coming in time to jump down and lean against the tree acting as if I were taking a nap. Because of wind noise, hearing aids were not compatible with riding a bike, so I did not wear them.

I'll come back tomorrow morning, I thought. *I'll wear my long pants, a ski mask, and a long-sleeved jersey, all dark, to hide any exposed skin.*

Following my GPS, I headed back out of the woods and onto the cart trail, which took me back to the road. I turned onto Riverside Drive and had a nice ride along the Scioto River heading south. A half hour later I was back at the motel. Had I continued riding another half hour, I would have been close to the Ohio State University campus.

"I'm going to send an e-mail to all our female classmates,"

96

Barbara said. "At least the ones that are left that I can find e-mail addresses for."

"Good idea," Jeannette responded. "I know Terry has a list and sends group e-mail jokes at least three times a day. We get a ton of 'em from Terry, and Rob hits the delete key them without opening them."

"I have those addresses because he sends me the same jokes," Barbara said. "I do the same thing Rob does. I found a lot more addresses on classmates.com so I'll add them to the ones I have and send out a mass warning."

"Make sure I get a copy," Jeannette said. "I'll print out a copy of your e-mail, compare the addresses to the class roster, and send out copies via snail mail to those not on the e-mail list."

"Okay," Barbara said. "See ya later."

"Bye," Jeannette said and hung up.

Barbara sent out the e-mail to 72 of the 148 female classmates that evening. The remaining 76 on the roster were either deceased, did not have an e-mail address on file, or there was no information on them at all.

Dear Classmates,

I am sending this to all the women to warn you of a potential danger. At least fifteen of our female classmates have been murdered in the past two years. It is not their deaths that are so alarming as it is the method of their demise. They have all been mutilated after death. Because of the manner in which they were murdered, the police believe that there is a serial killer involved. Our reunion committee believes that these were not random acts since all were our classmates. Therefore I am warning you to take appropriate action. This is not a hoax and if you have any questions, please call me on 330 823-5555. Please also e-mail me back with any changes to your e-mail accounts and those of others whom we might need to alert.

Thanks, and we'll keep you posted,

Barbara

One of the recipients was Angela, whose husband, Terry, saw it. He felt it was his duty to resend it to all on his class list-serve which I was on, and within seconds I had a copy in my inbox; however, I was in Columbus on "assignment."

This job would be similar to the first one he did on That Bitch. The north side of the house faced away from any other structure. There was a quarter mile of field sparsely filled with trees between the north side and the main road. This time, he would leave the body in the house, a note with a different kind of heart in the front yard, and would take the real heart with him. He had a special place he wanted her heart displayed and it was of no use to take the body with him too. This change in modus operandi would throw off his pursuers, at least until they found another note and the heart at Barbara's.

From his perch on the branch in the woods he watched patiently for three days. The man of the house dutifully left every weekday morning at just after 6:30. Janet left the house at almost the same time each day, late in the morning around 11:30, and returned at 1:30.

Probably some ladies' function at noon, he thought. *I'll just slip in while she's gone.*

He didn't see any animals through the windows or in the backyard. The yard was not fenced in, which might have indicated that they had a dog. They could have a cat, but surely it would have been catching some rays in the window on the west side of the house in the late afternoon sun. Cats were not a problem anyway. They would most likely just run and hide when a stranger entered. If not, he would make "friends" with them.

He decided Thursday would be the day and put all he needed into a backpack before his morning bike ride. It was raining lightly, but it was okay for him to ride in wet weather as long as he wore his rain gear. Rainy weather would also ensure that there would be no one on the golf course. No observers, no witnesses. Arriving a little after six in the morning, he waited at the base of the tree.

No use climbing up to my perch, he thought. *I'd just have to climb back down in fifteen minutes or so.*

This morning, however, the man of the house didn't leave at his usual time, so he sat down at the base of the tree at 7:00 and dozed off. He was awakened at 8:00 by the slam of a car door and aimed his binoculars toward the house.

"Police?" he wondered aloud. "What are they doing here?"

Rather than leave, his curiosity made him stay. Three people got out of the cruiser, one was in uniform. Of the two others, one was an older man, who he guessed was fifty or sixty and the other, a young woman carrying an umbrella. All three headed up the walk toward the entrance door. When the trio got to the door, it opened and Janet greeted them.

She still has those big boobs, he thought and then reminisced. Janet had been "well gifted" in high school. She had the boobs and a small waist which made them look even bigger. She had a pretty face. Not homecoming-queen pretty, but she sure was popular with the guys. Her last name had put them close together in the classroom where they all sat in alphabetical order. From junior high through all but the last year of high school, she was almost always in the desk in front of him, her long, shiny black hair resting on the top of his desk. Hair he wanted to reach out and caress, but was too afraid of getting caught. *Then what would she think of him?*

Because she sat in front of him, he was able to observe her and all the notes that were passed to and from the boys in the class. She was popular. She had more looks than brains, but was not stupid. He would melt when, before class started, she would turn to ask him a question about their assignment pressing her breasts against the front of his desk. He was always happy to answer, gazing into those big brown eyes. He felt stirring in his pants when she did that. This made him uncomfortable and he was always careful not to stand until the sensation subsided.

In their senior year, she was in business classes and he was in college prep, so she no longer was in any of his classes, but their lockers were side-by-side in the hall outside of the chemistry classroom. One day, she had turned into him by accident and rubbed those boobs up against his arm.

"I'm sorry," was all he was able to blurt out as he started to turn red. She softly touched his arm as if saying *it happens all the time. Don't worry about it.* But she did not look at him and said nothing. He hurried to his solid geometry class two doors down the hall, sat at his desk and didn't move until the class was over, thinking of nothing but her.

She seemed nice enough, but ignored him like all the rest of the girls. He had no money to go on dates. He didn't play football. He did okay grade wise, but was not one to "study with." For lunch the in-crowd went to a Main-Street diner, Heggy's, where they would sit, buy lunch or a shake, talk, and laugh.

They laughed about me and those like me, he thought, but he didn't know that for certain. *I am just taking revenge for all of the no-chance-in-hell guys. The guys I hung around with, like Ray, Adrian, Frank, and Winston. This one's for you guys.*

"Ma'am, are you Janet Gahtsum?" Ginny asked when the woman opened the door. She had already closed her umbrella and held it to the side. Water dripped off the end and fell on Jim's overly-shined oxford shoes.

"Yes," Janet responded. "Is something wrong?"

Everyone seemed to ask if there was something wrong when asked their names by the police. No one ever wanted to appear guilty or assume the cops were just being friendly. Ginny never heard 'oh, is this about the money I embezzled from the bank last year?' or 'yes, I'm fine, how are you, come on in and have a cup of coffee, and chat awhile.' But then, cops don't usually pay unannounced social calls.

"Since you're a graduate of the Alliance High class of sixty-two, we need to warn you of a possible threat to your life," Ginny said.

"Come on in and let me close the door," Janet said, backing away from the door, but keeping one hand on the knob. "I don't want to get all that humidity in the house."

Ginny set her umbrella down leaning it up against the side wall of the front portico entrance and all three went inside, wiping their shoes on the entrance mat.

"We won't be long Ms. Gahtsum," Ginny said.

They followed her to a glassed-in area straight ahead along the entrance hallway. They passed a living area on the left that looked unused and a formal dining area on the right, which was nicely adorned with solid cherry-wood furniture. When they sat down at the well-used table in the three-season room, Ginny handed her one of her cards and explained to Janet as much as she dared without compromising the investigation.

"I received an e-mail, rather my husband did on our joint account, just yesterday telling me the same thing, Janet said. "I didn't interrupt you because I wanted to see if it was the same information. I shrugged off the e-mail as a hoax as they wanted us to verify our e-mail account for future information. I don't trust the internet."

"I don't blame you, but the e-mail, as we have just verified, is legitimate," Ginny said. "So please be careful and feel free to call us at the number on my card." The three officers got up to leave.

"I sure will," Janet responded, as she too got up and led them back down the hallway.

When they exited the house, it was still raining lightly and Ginny grabbed and opened her umbrella before following the two men back to the cruiser.

The sound of the front door closing jarred me from my trance-like state. The cops had left the house and were walking back to the police cruiser. I still held the binoculars to my eyes, but glanced momentarily at the cell phone resting on the ground beside me. I didn't carry a watch and used the cell to tell the time. I had been sitting there staring at the house through the binoculars for almost a half hour, staring at the present but seeing the past, thinking about those boobs.

Before getting into the cruiser, the female took a look around and stared directly at me, but with my black clothing I should be blending into the shadowed trunk of the tall oak tree behind me. The bike was hidden, lying on its side deeper in the woods. It was dark, and there would be no glint of light coming from the no-glare glass of the binoculars. Still, something warned me that I might want to reconsider effecting an exorcism this day.

When she got into the cruiser and closed the door, Ginny asked, "Where do those woods go?"

"There's another row of houses on the other side," the uniformed officer said. "I believe there's a golf green in between here and those houses. I'll show you down at the end of this street." He started the cruiser, pulled straight ahead, and turned on the street going south. There was a dead end sign just as they turned. At the end of the road the woods narrowed to a line of one or two trees deep. A fairway was visible and on the other side was another group of trees with houses beyond.

"Drive back slowly," Ginny said. "I think I saw someone sitting up against a tree at the edge of the woods."

"Maybe it was just an abortion," Jim said.

The uniformed officer jerked his head back slightly as if tapped on the forehead with a hammer.

She knew he meant apparition, but said nothing to correct him. *Another Jimism,* she thought, *or was it drug damage?*

At least he didn't say "a fig newton of your image relation," for "figment of your imagination," which she had heard him say in similar situations.

As soon as the black and white headed toward the end of the dead-end street, I moved back deeper into the woods. I could still see the road from where I was and trained the binoculars to where the cops would have to pass by. They did, but when they were adjacent to where I had been sitting, they stopped and the plainclothes cops got out of the car. I moved deeper into the woods out of sight and back to where my bike was. As carefully as I could, I pushed my bike to the cart path and pedaled back to one of the residential streets. In seconds I was back out on the main road and in a few seconds more I was back on Riverside Drive heading for my truck.

"Somebody was definitely here," Ginny said. "Look at the way the weeds are lying flat around the base of this tree." It had stopped drizzling so she had left her umbrella in the car.

"It could have been an animal, maybe a dog or deer," Jim said.

"A dog, maybe," Ginny said. "What I saw was dark and a deer would have been more visible and brownish. An animal of the size I saw would probably have left some fur behind too."

"Should we call out the crime lab?" Jim asked.

"No crime has been committed," Ginny said. "We can't justify a team based on what I might have seen. It could have been someone hiking in the woods who just happened to be resting against this tree, saw us, and got curious."

"That's probably closer to the truth than fact," Jim said, first tugging at his mustache and then rubbing the thumb and index finger of his left hand along his jaw line lightly squeezing his chin forming a cleft like Kirk Douglas.

"Let's go," Ginny said, as it started to sprinkle again, a

little harder this time. With no umbrella to protect her from the drizzle, she didn't want to ruin a two-hundred dollar cut and set. When they got back to the cruiser the uniformed officer was leaning against the right front fender of the car finishing a cigarette which he held in a cupped, turned-under right hand to shield it from the rain.

"Could you have a black and white drive through this neighborhood at random intervals throughout the night?" Ginny asked as she hurriedly got into the black and white.

"Better take that up with the chief when we get back to the station," the uniformed officer said, snuffing out his cigarette on the sole of his plastic-looking uniform shoe. She didn't see what he did with the butt; however, it was not in his hands when he got back into the car. He reeked of smoke and she wished she had gotten into the back seat.

CHAPTER TWELVE

HE CAME BACK AFTER midnight, walking the five miles from where he had parked the truck in the parking lot of an all-night grocery store at the end of a strip mall. The skies had cleared and the moon was showing. The truck was under a large maple tree which shielded it from the parking lot light on the island across from the tree. He left Dedra alone in the cab with access through the rear sliding windows and to the bed of the camper where her litter box was. When he got to the housing area, the golf cart paths made it easy for him to work his way to the street to where his quarry was. He waited until the black and white had left the area, and then proceeded to the south side of the house. The window to the garage was facing the neighbor's fence and couldn't be seen from the street.

There were security alarm warning signs on the side yard of the house which he had been watching the last three days. There was an alarm-company sticker on the garage window too. Most home owners relied on motion detectors rather than glass or window sensors to set off the alarm system. There were two cars in the garage so he was sure they were both home.

If they armed the system at night, only the perimeter entry doors would be set. The motion detectors would be off to keep occupants from setting off the alarm.

Using a jimmy to unlatch the garage window, he slid the window open and crawled through. *So far so good*, he thought. As he had done at That Bitch's house, he pried on the upper door stop until a gap was formed allowing him to slide a metal plate between the door and the jamb. He pulled the pry bar away from the jamb and the header held the metal plate in place. He turned the door knob and found it unlocked. He could hear the faint sound of what must have been a TV. He looked up at the door jamb and noticed that the door switch was not magnetic, but a detent ball. It was a spring loaded little ball that moved down and completed a circuit when the door was opened. This type of trip device was more prone to false alarms because of vibration or door movement caused by wind. The temporary magnetic plate he used defeated both magnetic and detent ball systems.

The sound of a TV drew him to a family room. There on a reclining sofa, stretched out to an almost horizontal position, was a man. The top of his balding head could be seen and it was obvious that he was asleep, or at least had his eyes closed. The TV was on to the *Godfather*, a movie he had seen at least five times and he could have sat down and watched it again, but he had a job to do.

His stun gun was out and armed. From behind, he carefully lifted the blanket that covered the man in the area over his heart. The man stirred slightly just as he touched the probes to his pajama-covered chest. When he pushed the button, the man jerked slightly and then relaxed totally as if he had fallen into a deep sleep. There was no loud crackle as the nearly one-million volt charge went through the flesh and paralyzed the muscles around the heart, and most likely, the heart muscles too. The sound of miniature lightening bolts only occurred when the gun was tested in open air without touching any conducting objects.

Keeping the stun gun on the man's chest he held down the "on" button for the count of ten. The instructions that had come with the gun cautioned against holding it against someone for this long, but he didn't want the man to get up for a while.

Phase two complete, he thought, as he took his thumb off the button and lifted the gun from the man.

Just when he turned around to locate the woman, he stopped cold. There was a shadow moving across the floor in the dim light of the adjoining room off the kitchen. He had noticed the nightlight as he had come in from the garage. *Someone was up.*

As the sound of running water reached him, he moved back into the shadows in the corner of the room. He crouched low with the stun gun at the ready as she came into view carrying a glass of water. She was in a pair of loose, light-blue pajamas, big enough to be the man's. She stopped for a second and took a sip of water eyeing the movie as if she were enjoying the scene. She, too, must have seen the movie several times as she spoke along with Don Corleone when he uttered "I'll make him an offer he can't refuse."

She walked over to the man and with her free hand, gingerly replaced the corner of the blanket over his heart, the corner he had just removed seconds earlier. She then gently kissed him on the bald pate of his head. Turning away from the dark shadow in the corner, she ambled back toward the kitchen area, her shadow disappearing with her. She stopped momentarily to check that the alarm system was on.

After waiting a few minutes until his heartbeat returned to normal, he headed back the way she had gone. As he passed the kitchen counter, he noticed a brown, plastic bottle of pills on the counter and picked them up.

Ambien CR! He had seen enough TV commercials to know they were sleeping pills. *Had she taken them, or had the man?* He decided to go back out to the family room and watch some of the movie and let the drugs take effect, in case it was her.

When the movie producer pulled back the sheet to reveal the gruesome horse's head with all the associated blood, he got up from the couch. *I wonder what type of sleeping pills the man in the movie could have taken back in the 50's to be able to sleep through someone putting a bleeding horse's head under the sheets he was lying on?* he thought.

Shrugging his shoulders, he decided to give the man another jolt. Uncovering his chest again, he jabbed the pen down and pushed the button. There was no reaction from the man this time, which is what he thought would happen, or wouldn't. He headed back out to the kitchen and followed the corridor toward the back of the house.

At the end of the hallway were three rooms, two on his right and one on his left. He peered around the corner of the one on his left. There she was, lying on her left side facing away from him. The nearly empty glass of water was on the night stand directly in front of her. Stealing quietly around to her side of the bed, in the pale illumination from the security light in the back yard, he saw that she was in a deep sleep state. There was no REM visible from behind her eyelids which indicated she was not dreaming. Instead of going for the heart, which he didn't want to stop from bleeding, he placed the pen on the side of her neck and pushed the button. As with the man, she jerked once, and then went limp. A count of ten later, he lifted the pen and saw two red welts where the lightning had penetrated the skin. He would have to do something about that piece of evidence.

He pulled back the sheets and rolled the body onto its back. He then took the knife and the chest spreader from his tool belt and began the gruesome task of getting to her heart. As he cracked the chest, he saw the object of his quest. It was still beating, but ever so slightly. Blood was pouring from the gaping wound he had made and the heart must have been winding down from the lack of blood. The surgical gloves he wore kept him from coming in contact with the blood directly, but, as with a surgeon, they didn't hamper him in any way.

Blood had pooled on and around her now lifeless body as phase three was accomplished. He placed the now-still heart in a large sandwich bag and tucked it into the pouch on the side of his cargo pants. He left the chest spreader, he had others, and wiped the knife as clean as he could on the pulled back sheet. He noticed that it was silk, just like the sheets covering the dead horse head. After he cut a piece from her neck and placed it in the other pouch on his pants, he rolled the body onto its side, facing him, and covered it up.

When they find her body, It will be just like the Godfather scene in the producer's bedroom, he thought. *Only she won't be uncovering herself.* As she had done to the man, he bent down and kissed her on the still-warm forehead. He did so carefully, so as not to leave any DNA containing saliva, and then left the room. He exited through the garage door. After closing the door, he removed the metal plate he had placed to thwart the entrance alarm. He left through the still open window and ducked behind a bush as the squad car made a slow pass on the north side of the house. When it had left the housing area, he retrieved a package from under a bush where he had placed it before opening the window. He took the package to the front yard, opened the package, spread out the marked paper, and carved a jagged corner from the item that had been in the package. Having finished phase four, he crossed the road and walked back the way he had come.

When he got back to the truck, he opened the driver's side rear door and set the present for Barbara on the floor. Dedra jumped to the floor from her resting place on the rear bench seat and approached the package with natural curiosity. She sniffed at it and tilted her head looking at him as if asking, 'another one?' She then jumped back up onto the seat and curled up for another catnap.

He hadn't noticed the squad car parked in the shadows at the far end of the parking lot pointed in his direction, but they noticed him. As he pulled away from the parking space, the squad car started toward him.

"That outa state truck don't look like it belongs here," Officer Barney said to his partner. "Let's pull him over and ask a few questions." A rash of burglaries in the area prompted the police to be on the alert for suspicious vehicles.

"Yeah," Andy, the other cop, said. "I'd like to know what that was he took out of his pants and put in the back seat. All the stores except for the donut shop are closed and he didn't come from that direction."

As he headed toward the exit at the side of one of the stores, Dedra suddenly jumped up onto the passenger's side seat acting agitated.

"What's wrong girl?" he said, turning his head toward the squad car. "Oh, I see! We're being followed. Thanks for the warning."

The building blocked the cruiser's line-of-sight of the truck when he headed toward the side exit. Instead of using the parking lot exit to his left, he continued straight ahead toward the alleyway behind the stores where delivery trucks went to offload supplies. Taking a quick right turn, he sped along the alley which had a high grass-covered bank to the left. Had the hill been a little flatter he would have put the truck into four-wheel drive and ducked into the cover of the woods. There were trees, but not close enough together to impede passage.

"Where'd he go?" Barney blurted out as the squad car rounded the corner of the building.

"He's runnin' through the back of the buildings," Andy said, pointing the way. "I'm callin' for backup."

"Dedra, do your magic and make them disappear," he said to the cat who was on her hind legs front paws on the top of the passenger side bucket seat, peering behind them back down the alley. In the rearview mirror, he could see the lights of the squad car bouncing off the high bank as it approached the entrance to the alley. The cat got on all fours and let out a loud "marawal," arching its back at the same time. Before the pursuing police could turn the sharp corner, the truck jerked toward the left and he found himself turning right to compensate. His tunnel vision returned.

"What?" Andy said in disbelief as they made the turn. The alley was straight with solid walls on the right and an almost ninety-degree bank on the left. The way they had come in and the exit a quarter mile ahead of them were the only two ways in or out. There were no other vehicles in sight. Barney slammed on the brakes and threw the cruiser into reverse causing Andy to reach out and put his hands on the dashboard to brace himself.

"Ya think he got all the way to the end already?" Andy asked. "He'd had ta have a rocket up his ass."

His right arm draped over the rear of the seat and head turned looking toward the back of the cruiser, Barney responded, "I just wanna check to make sure." He backed all the way to the front parking lot and jammed on the brakes. They both glared at the street on the other end of the strip but saw nothing. They watched for a couple of minutes before Barney put the car back into drive and went around to the back of the store.

Neither one of them said a word as Barney quickly drove the length of the alley, exiting on the other side. After a few minutes, Barney said, "Let's cruise around this area awhile and see if we can spot the truck and then head on over to the neighborhood we're supposed to be watching. Call his license plate number in and see if they can ID the owner."

"Will do," Andy responded.

I was already heading north on old Route 62 when Andy and Barney found out that the plates had been reported stolen. U.S. Route 62 was commissioned in 1930 and began at Niagara Falls, New York and was completed in 1944, stopping in El Paso, Texas. A lot of little towns were connected along its two-thousand mile length. Upon completion of the interstate system, the road was not used very much, but was still there. I was not in any hurry and wanted to avoid any busy highways, so I took the less-traveled route.

"Go ahead and do your thing, Dedra," he told the cat. "Take us back to our world." When he got control of the truck again, he pulled onto a side road and changed the license plates, burying the old ones in a ditch. He then pulled back onto Route 62 and headed for Alliance.

CHAPTER THIRTEEN

"THE PATROLMAN FOUND THE open garage door window around eleven-thirty this morning after he got suspicious." Jim said. "The morning paper was not picked up as they had always done, and no one had seen her husband leave the house. He called in for backup then entered through the window. The rest you know."

"So now we have a possible double homicide," Ginny said. "Her husband's death is suspicious even though the coroner ruled it a heart attack in his preliminary report at the scene."

"He found two sets of little red marks on the chest area just above the heart." Jim countered. "We don't know what caused them, but it could have been from the man clawing at his chest if he had chest pains. There were no such marks on her body, but it was so badly mutilated around the heart that none would have been seen anyway. Goddamn mess in the bedroom, at least on the bed. The heart hasn't been found and we suspect the perp took it with him."

They were standing over the package spread out on the

lawn. It was a heart-shaped, hollowed-out, pink-colored item. It could have been a large Valentine's Day gift if it hadn't been for the gruesome way it was displayed. The bottom right corner had a hole cut away made to look as if it had been bitten into by human teeth. Running out from the hole was a red, sticky looking substance the consistency of congealed blood. Under the item was a standard sheet of paper with groups of numbers on it.

"We've seen that before," Ginny said. "I wonder why he didn't leave the real heart as he did before?"

"Maybe we have a copycat killer at work," Jim offered.

"Somehow I don't think so." Ginny replied. "I think it's our friend at work again. You said the alarm went off when the patrolman entered the house?"

"Yes, everything was set as if the perp disarmed and then rearmed the system before he or she left. We did find that the jamb had been pried loose in the vicinity of the garage door alarm switch. We don't know when the jamb had been damaged, but my guess is whoever did this knows how to defeat a house alarm."

"That sounds familiar," Ginny said. "We'll have to check and double check the similarities between this and the other cases. See if the numbers on the paper make any sense using the code we have."

"It'll be awhile before we get all the goo cleaned off it so we can get to all the numbers."

"Any idea what that red stuff is?"

"It looks like cherry pie filling without the cherries, but no one is willing to taste it to find out," Jim said.

"We'll just have to wait for the lab results, but I'll bet you're right," Ginny said.

"I'd rather be correct than sorry," Jim mis-quipped.

He had the real heart back in his truck and was going to give Barbara a special package. He kept it under ice in the ice chest to keep it from spoiling too quickly. When he got to his motel room, he booted up his computer and checked his e-mail.

"So that's why the cops were all around the place," he said aloud. "Good ol' Barbara has cracked the code and warned all the classmates."

"We've got the translation," Jim said, showing Ginny the piece of paper.

29	21	21	23	0
31	4	4	31	0
31	21	21	17	0
0	0	0	0	0
31	20	22	13	0
31	21	21	17	0
31	20	20	31	0
31	1	1	1	0
31	1	1	1	0
16	8	7	8	16
0	0	0	0	0
16	8	16	8	16
31	20	20	31	0
29	21	21	23	0
0	0	0	0	0
31	8	4	2	31
31	0	0	0	0
31	17	17	17	0
31	21	21	17	0
0	0	0	0	0
16	16	31	16	16
31	17	17	31	0
0	0	0	0	0
31	8	4	4	31
31	21	21	17	0

"Well what's it mean?" she asked.

"If the code is right, it reads 'she really was nice to me.'"

"That doesn't make sense," Ginny said. "What the hell does that mean?"

"Maybe it means something to him."

"Or to someone else," she added.

"Why don't we send it to that Chief Diarrhea in Alliance," Jim offered

"You mean Dorian," she corrected. "Yeah, do that and see if anyone has a clue what it means."

"Yeah! Maybe he can help us put the horse in front of the apple cart."

When Chief Dorian received the fax, it was already too late.

He wasted no time in getting to Alliance with his treat for Barbara. Since he had seen that they had the code, or at least thought they did, they might also have found what all the murdered women had in common.

The "present" he had for her would have to be left where Charro couldn't bother it. It wouldn't take him long to devour a tasty morsel such as a heart. To a dog his size the heart would be like a snack, just a couple of bites and a swallow.

The last time he had paid her a visit, he had left no clues that anyone had been there and this time would be no different. During that visit, he had taken a small box which had been used previously to mail her something from an on-line purchase. The Amazon.com logo was on two sides of the box, and a mailing label with her address was on the top. He would just put her present inside, tape it closed, and lay it on the front porch as if the mail carrier had brought it.

Her house was only three doors up the street from the country club parking lot so that is where he parked the truck. He walked up and placed the package on the front porch. As he was walking away he heard the door open.

"Can I help you?" a female voice offered from the direction of the house.

He almost took off running, but the voice was that of a younger woman. She probably didn't know all her neighbors and he took that chance by responding. He smiled as if he were one of her friendly neighbors.

"No, I just brought that package down. I live up the street and it was mis-delivered to our house. Have a nice day."

"Oh thank you," the blonde woman said. She couldn't be more than thirty, if that old. He smiled again, waved 'bye to her, and walked west although the parking lot was east.

She picked up the package and took it into the house. He continued to the next street, turned north, went to the first alley and cut back east to his truck. He was out of town five minutes later.

When Barbara got back from her walk with Charro, she took off his leash as she went through the gate leading to her cottage behind the main house. Leaving the dog in the fenced-in yard, she went back through the gate and closing it behind her went to the main house to get her mail. She usually only checked it once a week, but she was expecting the delivery of an item she had recently purchased online.

When she returned, Charro was dutifully waiting for his "mama" inside the fenced in area which surrounded the cottage on three sides. He could have easily jumped the short side of the fence, it was only two-feet high, but he never had. He was content to just rest his chin on the top of the fence and look forlornly toward her. As she usually did, she stepped over the fence with her mail in hand and started heading for the cottage. Charro pressed his nose up against the box and tried to bite into it.

"Not for you," she said, but the dog persisted. When he continued trying to get the box, she reprimanded him with a stern, "No!"

This seemed to work as he bounded off for the cottage stopping on the porch in front of the door. She opened the door and let him in. He usually headed for his water bowl to lap continuously at the water, but this time he got five feet inside the door and sat as if he were expecting a treat.

"You ate them all," she said, referring to the snacks she carried with her on her long walks with him. She was able to train him to walk beside her with a tug of the leash, a command, and then a treat when he obeyed. She set the package, the rest of the mail on top of it, on the small table to the right of the door. Immediately Charro was up and nosing it. He was acting so agitated, that she grabbed him by the collar and led him to the bedroom and closed the door, trapping him inside.

She retrieved a knife from the kitchen and returned to the living room to open the package. Seconds later she dialed 911.

Chief Dorian held the heart for the team from Columbus who started for Alliance a half hour after he had called them.

"We do have a cadaver with a missing heart here," Ginny told the chief when he had called. "The victim was one of the women in the Columbus area we had warned who had attended Alliance High School and graduated in 1962, the same year as the others. We'll be there as soon as we can to get some DNA to compare with our body and talk to the woman who found the package."

"Okay," the chief replied, "but you realize I can't let it out of my control until it's proven to be from your victim."

"Of course," Ginny said. "We wouldn't expect you to, but hopefully you will work with us on this should it prove to belong to our victim."

"I would be happy to," he said, again thinking about all the free publicity this would give him in his upcoming bid for sheriff of Stark County. "I'll see if the two witnesses who received the package will be available to talk to you. I'm heading over to the scene to talk to them myself, while things are still fresh."

"Depending on what you find, we might not need to talk to them too," Ginny said.

Two weeks later, the Columbus police had received DNA results indicating that the heart belonged to Jenny.

"Chief," Ginny said. "We have confirmation that the heart belongs to our victim."

"Well, we suspected that much, didn't we?" Chief responded. "I'll arrange for the heart to be transferred to your jurisdiction and you can have it today if you want."

"Tomorrow will be fine," Ginny said, amazed at how quickly small towns can react. *It would have taken a week to transfer evidence in Columbus*, she thought, but would not say that to the chief.

Reacting on a hunch that the victims from the class of '62 graduating class all knew their killer, and that he was a member of the same class, the chief decided to show Brandy the annual yearbook. She was the one who had seen the-so called neighbor who delivered the package to the front door. The chief's detectives had interviewed every neighbor in the vicinity and none had claimed to have been that person. The mailman remembered delivering five packages on Barbara's and adjacent streets that day, and all of them had been accounted for.

"I don't see anyone that looks like him," Brandy said. She had just finished looking at the pictures of all the 1962 graduates.

"Look at these yearbooks from Marlington and West Branch," the chief said. He was assisting with this investigation himself in the hopes that his department could find the suspect. The *Today* show was now following the case with interest and a spot on the morning news show could be in the offing. The other two high schools' yearbooks also turned up nothing.

"I have the prior-year books," Barbara said. "Maybe he left school to join the army as some others did before they graduated, or didn't get his picture taken. He may also have been set back a grade or two."

Schools back in the fifties would set a student back a grade or two for poor performance. It was incentive for students to do at least well enough to keep up with their friends. Schools don't do that as much anymore.

"Yeah," Chief said. "Where are they?"

"At my place," she said as she headed for her cottage. She returned less than five minutes later. She opened the books to her class pictures and handed them to Brandy.

"That looks like him," Brandy said, pointing to a picture in the 1960 yearbook on the very first group of pictures. "I can't be sure because this is such an old picture, but yeah, he had the same eyes and mouth."

"I think there's a later picture of him in the1962 yearbook," Barbara said.

"But I looked at them all and don't remember seeing that name," Brandy said.

"Let me look," Barbara said, already thumbing her way past the individual pictures. "I think he was in one of the group club photos, maybe Science club or Spanish Club. He took three years of Spanish and was interested in math and science. Here it is!" She handed the book to Brandy who looked intently at the picture."

"Yes!" she said. "That definitely could be him."

"Are you sure?" the chief asked, not wanting to base any conclusions on "definitely-could-be" testimony.

"I believe he was at one of the reunions too," Barbara said. "Maybe the twenty-fifth or thirtieth. I have those pictures here too." She pulled two eight by ten color pictures out of a manila envelope.

"Oh, that's him," Brandy said, pointing to a man in the back row of the twenty-fifth reunion group shot. "And here he is again." She was pointing to the same man in the thirtieth reunion picture this time. "The same guy, I'm sure of it."

"Well," the chief said. "Finally we have a name and a face. There's my little code breaker," he added as David came in from playing adult-organized baseball.

"What are you doing?" David asked.

"Gathering evidence," the Chief said. "Gathering evidence."

Later that day, he intercepted her e-mail describing what had happened and naming him as the prime suspect.

So, they suspect that it is I, he thought. *I was afraid they could ID me after that woman, Brandy, the e-mail said her name was, spotted me delivering the package. Looks like I need to make a trip down to Padre Island and hide out on the beach awhile. No one will suspect that's where I am.*

As he was heading for the Texas coast, Chief Dorian, with the task force from Columbus, was briefing the FBI on all the evidence they had collected so far.

"His last-known address is in Vermont, but he doesn't live there anymore," Chief said. "He was in the Dallas and Corpus Christi areas in Texas before that. Someone seems to remember he lived in Japan, but where he lives now is unknown. He worked with a company called Macon Engineering, but not since 1996. His boss said his wife was killed in the crash of TWA Flight 800, but there is no record of her being on the flight, and no one knows where he's been since he was given time off from work to grieve."

"What about a driver's license, car registration, all that?" the FBI agent asked.

"His Vermont driver's license and plates are still good, but he hasn't renewed the annual sticker on his truck, assuming he still has the same vehicle. This guy is just invisible on the radar. We've got an all-points on him and he's been entered into the database, so if he turns up somewhere we'll be notified."

"There's not much we can do until then, is there?" the

agent asked. "What about potential victims?"

"They've all been notified," Chief answered. "The one's that are left, that is."

In Oklahoma City, he picked up I-35 and headed south toward Dallas. "We'll be in San Antone for breakfast, Dedra," he said aloud. "Then it's just a short hop to Corpus and the serenity of Padre Island."

Dedra looked at him with those wide open eyes, and he felt a tear well up in him remembering another cat, his beloved wife Dee, and the wonderful short period of time they shared. "I sure wish I could be with her again," he said, wiping the tears off his cheeks. He remembered what his mother had told him as a child.

"Be careful what you wish for," she had said. "Trust in God and be happy with what you've already got."

It was a bright and sunny morning as he crossed the bridge on South Padre Island Drive. At the top of the bridge he could see far out into the gulf to the southeast. He passed a country club and condos and continued south on Padre Island National Seashore. Passing the four-wheel-drive–only-beyond-this-point sign, he pushed the button on his dash for auto four-wheel drive. The light on the button flashed a couple of times and then turned a steady orange indicating it was in auto four-wheel. The sand was packed hard, but if he hit a soft area, the transmission would sense any slippage and engage the front wheels within a millisecond.

Dedra was alert at her perch on the dash. Her eyes were wide and she seemed to be absorbing the heat from the sun and watching all the seagulls. The last exit in Corpus was the Flour Bluff area adjacent to the Naval Air Station and Army Depot where helicopters for the army were maintained and repaired. It was also a training facility for helicopter pilots and naval aviators. He could see the helicopters flying their morning missions off to the left. Flour Bluff was where he had stopped at a convenience store to top off the fuel tank and get supplies to last him a few days. That's when he was spotted.

The man working behind the counter was a retired police officer with friends still on the force. They got together at least twice a week at the local Black Hawk Bar to reminisce about past cases and talk about on-going investigations. Two nights before, they had talked about an all-points on a suspected serial killer with ties to the Corpus area. They had described the suspect along with the details of the gruesome killings.

When he saw the man who fit the description come into his store and stock up on food, water, dog, and cat food, he called one of his buddies. While on duty later that morning the cop buddy brought by a picture of the suspect and the clerk confirmed his identity.

"That sure looks like him," the clerk said. "He bought enough food for at least a week. He bought cat food and all the large bags of dog food we had. When he left he headed south toward the bridge."

"Sounds like he's going to spend some time on the island," his buddy said. "Thanks for keepin' your eyes open and lettin' me know. I owe ya one."

"I'll take ya up on that the next time we're at the Hawk," the clerk said.

"You're on."

As soon as they were notified, the FBI had a couple of agents talking to the commander at the air station. They were able to get a helicopter to fly them along the beach, all the way to Mexico if necessary, in hopes of spotting the suspect's truck. Speed was essential. Two mornings after he was spotted at the convenience store, the agents were strapped in and lifting off from the helipad next to Hangar 21.

"First time in a helicopter?" the pilot asked. The pilot was a civilian, who had served in Desert Storm and taken the job of test flying helicopters when he got out of the military. He would be retiring this year after thirty-two years, including his tour of duty in the army. Only one of the agents answered. The other was taking a white knuckle flight.

"No," the agent said. "But George there hasn't been in one yet. He doesn't even like to fly in a fixed-wing aircraft."

"This should be a gentle flight," the pilot said. "Winds are coming off the water and are light and variable. We'll be flying just off the beach at about a thousand feet."

In his younger days he would have given his passengers something to talk about; flying low, flying sideways, dropping and rising swiftly, but he had mellowed and become sympathetic with age. Also, he might have to clean up any failure on their part in being able to grab an airsickness bag fast enough. The smell of puke in a cockpit is not a good way to start the day either.

"If we spot him, can we set down?" the not-so-sick agent asked.

"We could, but backwash would kick up the sand something fierce and get sucked into the intake. This bird was just overhauled and doesn't need to be torn apart again. I was told we were just going to locate the truck and then radio its location back to the base."

"We want this guy badly, but if he doesn't suspect we're looking for him, we'll have enough time to drive back out here," the agent said. "If we spot him, just keep going until we're far enough to turn around and head back over land. That way he'll think this is just a routine test flight."

"It depends on how far south he is. We don't fly all the way to Mexico when we go out on test flights. My guess is he's this side of the fish pass."

"Fish pass?"

"Yeah. There's a fish pass at the end of the National Sea Shore at Port Mansfield about seventy-five miles south. It's a channel across the island to allow fish to go from the gulf to the inland bay. It's pretty deep and can't be driven across. He can't go beyond that and unless he has a boat, there is only one way back and that's the way ya go in."

"No other bridges?" the agent asked.

"No, not until you get to Brownsville and the fish pass is about halfway between Corpus and there. If he's spotted and you have to drive out to get him, you'll need a four-wheel drive to get past the paved part."

"That can be arranged," the agent said.

"Yeah," the pilot said. "If we don't have one available at the base, there are rentals all over Corpus."

He heard the helicopter coming, but that was not unusual. They flew all along here on their test flights from the depot. Sometimes, in addition to the army choppers, there were Coast Guard helicopters just doing their fly-bys. But just to be sure, he grabbed his binoculars and sat up on the back of his open tailgate.

"That's interesting," he said aloud. Dedra was sprawled out on the bed of the truck watching a flock of seagulls sitting at the water's edge all facing into the wind. She didn't bother the seagulls which can get nasty sometimes. Seagulls didn't like dogs of any kind, but a cat was something that could be dive bombed and pecked at if necessary.

He noticed that there were two people in the front of the helicopter and maybe more in the back. The one in the copilot's seat was wearing a white shirt and tie. As they got closer, he pointed and turned his head as if to speak to someone behind him, then reached over his left shoulder and brought back a pair of binoculars.

"So, they're looking for someone," he said. He crawled back into the bed of the truck and continued to observe through the tinted Plexiglas of the camper top. As the helicopter got closer, he caught a glimpse of the back-seat passenger leaning forward for a better view. He had on a suit and from his left front pocket, a badge of some sort dangled. The helicopter moved a little closer to the shoreline, but didn't slow up at all. As they got closer, the man in the front kept the binoculars trained on his truck the entire time. He then handed the binoculars to the other man in the back seat, took a pad out of his shirt pocket and wrote something on it. The man in the back watched from the side window as the helicopter passed by and continued south along the shoreline.

"That definitely was not a routine test flight, Dedra. I think we had better be prepared for visitors." He kept hidden until he couldn't hear the helicopter anymore. He was listening for the helicopter to come back heading north, but it never came. Around noon, he felt safe enough to do some tunneling with the seagulls.

"Let's feed the gulls," he said to Dedra

Putting on a hooded shirt, he loaded up his pockets with dog food and took the nearly empty bag in his left hand. He left the hood down, forming a pocket behind him. The sun had gone behind some clouds, so it had cooled off considerably. Hoisting Dedra onto his shoulder so that she could rest her hind legs inside the hood, he headed for the shoreline. The wind was coming from the north so he walked in that direction. The gulls knew what was next as he had done this twice a day for the last three days. As he turned into the wind, the gulls started flying in behind him, squawking as loudly as they could. The noise only brought more gulls and soon they were flying behind him and on both sides. Dedra was moving from one of his shoulders to the other.

Waiting until the gulls were squawking at a frenzied pitch, he started to feed them by tossing dog food into the air and dropping some behind him. They were now at arms reach so he held out some food in his open palm. The gulls pecked his open hands to get the morsels. Some flew so close to him that their wings beat against his head and shoulders. Dedra was having a ball batting harmlessly at the screeching birds that were swooping and diving all around them. He had walked about a mile trailing the birds behind him when he noticed a dot way up on the island. He was on a portion of the beach that bent to the east so he could easily see at least five miles ahead.

He squinted to see through the mist caused by the waves breaking on shore. It looked like a Hummer, one of the smaller ones that were made for consumers rather than the army. He turned and noticed that he was a long way from his truck and would not be able to make it back before the Hummer reached him. He decided to just keep going at a slower pace. If there was trouble he would get Dedra to do her magic and they would slip through a seam into their parallel world. He had a lot of dog food left, so he kept feeding the gulls. He was just a tourist taking a walk along the beach with his cat, feeding the critters.

The Hummer hesitated as it approached him. The driver looked like the man in the helicopter and was wearing a white shirt, but no tie. He waved to them as they passed by. They were staring intently at him and his cat with their entourage of seagulls.

"Dedra, the one in the passenger seat was the one in the back of the helicopter," he said to the cat. "He still has his jacket on with the badge hanging out of the pocket."

"That must have been him," the agent-in-charge said. "That's what he was buying the dog food for, to feed the gulls."

"Yeah, and there was a cat on his back," his partner replied. "That fits with his buying the cat food too."

When the agents got to his truck, they verified that it fit the description of the same extended cab Chevy that had seemed to disappear in the strip mall parking lot in Ohio.

"Let's go ask him a few questions," the agent-in-charge said. They turned their Hummer and headed in his direction.

He turned around and headed back toward his truck and in the same direction that the Hummer had been going. It was harder to feed the gulls walking with the wind. They no longer were able to glide on the breeze. Instead, the birds had to fly in front of him and close to his side.

"Well Dedra," he said, "looks like we're in for some company. Are you ready to do your magic thing?"

Dedra stopped looking at the gulls and crawled up onto his shoulder. As the Hummer approached, now within one-hundred yards of them and moving fast, he stopped and tossed the rest of the dog food on the sand ahead of them. The din was deafening as scores of hungry gulls flocked in front of them coming from all directions.

"Now Dedra, now!" he said. The tunnel vision started.

The approaching Hummer disappeared behind a wall of seagulls as he too disappeared from their view.

"Be careful, he might be armed," the agent-in-charge said as they watched him disappear behind the birds.

"Yeah," his partner responded. "He might use the gulls as a shield while he draws his gun."

Thirty feet from where they had last seen him, the partner jammed on the brakes of the Hummer.

"He must be using them for cover," the agent-in-charge said, as they slid by and around the gulls. "Get out and go around the other side while I guard this side, and be careful." The agent-in-charge jumped out of the Hummer as it slid to a stop on the wet sand.

"You don't have to tell me that," his partner said. He drew his weapon and exited the driver's side. The birds looked like a feathery tornado and sounded as loud as a real twister as each bird tried to get to the pile of food on the sand.

"Where the fuck did he go?" the agent-in-charge said from the other side of the birds. "Fire your weapon and get these fuckin' birds outa here!"

There was a loud report as his partner fired his weapon harmlessly out into the bay. The birds immediately scattered in all directions at the loud sound. The agents were left staring at each other across a bird shit and dog food covered beach. They both immediately turned toward the bay, but there wasn't a ripple anywhere indicating that someone had taken cover underwater.

They circled around in opposite directions looking for signs of his having been there, and then at the sand for footprints.

"Here's where we last saw him," the agent-in-charge said, pointing at the footprints with his gun. "Everything else around these last two sets of prints is just seagull footprints, dog food, and shit." The gentle waves washing in from the gulf obliterated any markings further up the beach. "Ya can't even see where he walked before here."

They both holstered their weapons and walked around one more time looking at the beach and shaking their heads.

"We both saw him, didn't we?" the agent-in-charge asked.

"Yeah, but I ain't writin' this fuckin' report," his partner said. "I'll sign whatever you want, but I won't be able to put this down on paper."

They turned their attention toward the truck. It was still there, so they got back in the Hummer, turned it around and headed cautiously back down the beach. The seagulls returned to the remaining pile of dog food and before the two agents reached the truck, the birds had the area cleaned of any food.

"Well, Dedra, we did it again," he said, reaching over his right shoulder to pet the cat, but felt nothing. His truck was also gone as were the agents and their Hummer.

He spun around to see if Dedra had fallen out of the hood. Only the cat was not there. Instead, "she" was there.

Dee was standing right behind him as if reincarnated from Dedra. She was wet and her hair was straight and dripping. She was naked and looked as beautiful as she had the last time he had seen her that way, the night before she and her daughter, the human Dedra, had left for Paris.

"Dee!" he exclaimed. "Dee! Oh baby, I have missed you so much."

Tears streamed from his eyes and started pouring down his cheeks as she reached out to take his hand. She said nothing, but started walking toward the water. He followed, willingly. His love for her was so deep he didn't care where he was going as long as it was with her.

When they were in hip-deep water, Dee turned to him and put her arm around his waist. She rested her head on his shoulder as they continued deeper into the bay. He tilted his head and rested it on top of hers. Neck deep in the water, she turned to him, embraced him, and they started kissing. Being shorter than he, she was now floating in the water so he continued carrying her deeper. They were both floating now and the surface was just a shimmer above.

"God forgive me," were his last words.

He had gotten his wish. They were together again…this time, forever.

Chapter Fourteen

I watched as they towed the truck back toward the north end of the island. I also watched as helicopters searched up and down the shore.

"They must be looking from Corpus Christi to Mexico," I said aloud. "They won't find him."

I hauled in the un-baited fishing line and pulled up the anchor on the small fishing boat I had rented for the week. I was a mile off shore using binoculars to spy on all the proceedings on the beach. I was thinking about how I would need to update the class roster and the page that listed the deceased members. There were at least fifteen more names to add—at least fifteen—maybe more by the end of the year.

"I wonder if the seagulls in the Cayman Islands like dog food?" I asked the cat resting on the cushioned seat next to me. She looked up as the motor spluttered to life and I sat back down and aimed the bow of the boat for the coast north of Corpus.

The agent's report indicated that the suspect must have

escaped behind some sand dunes unseen by them and somehow made it off the island without a trace. No one would believe what they had really observed.

The truck, hauled to a hangar at the air station, was later taken by flatbed to a crime lab where traces of some of the victims were found. In the back of the truck was discovered a coded message, handwritten this time, and wet with salt water.

31	4	4	31	0
31	21	21	17	0
0	0	0	0	0
31	0	0	0	0
29	21	21	23	0
0	0	0	0	0
16	8	16	8	16
31	0	0	0	0
16	16	31	16	16
31	4	4	31	0
0	0	0	0	0
31	8	4	4	31
31	21	21	17	0
0	4	4	4	0
31	8	4	2	31
31	17	17	31	0
16	8	16	8	16
0	0	0	0	0
31	17	17	14	0
31	21	21	17	0
31	21	21	17	0
192	256	285	288	192

He remains one of the FBI's Most Wanted, keeping his remaining female graduating classmates waiting and worrying – for the rest of their lives.

EPILOG

"HOW IS OUR PATIENT doing?" Dr. Merkin asked. "Is he still hallucinating?" The doctor was the head of the psychiatric ward at Houston General Hospital where the unknown person had been brought. The man had been found in a small fishing boat drifting off shore near Galveston on the gulf coast about forty miles from the hospital. The disheveled man was incoherent, suffering from exposure, and hallucinating. There was no identification as to who he was. The authorities had no matching missing person's reports which would help to give him at least a name.

"He still acts as if someone or something is talking to him and reaches for objects as if they're too far away to grab," the ward nurse replied. "He also keeps talking to a something or someone that he calls Dedra, and pretends to give her some of his food by placing it on the sheets by his feet. The rest of the time he just stares out into space and doesn't acknowledge anyone. He's nonviolent, so we don't have him on any of the as-needed psychotic or tranquilizing drugs which you prescribed. He has recovered from the exposure, except for the Dedra episodes, eats normally when food is placed on his tray, and is non ambulatory. We still have no idea who he is or where he comes from, and we may never find out."

"We've obtained a court order appointing a lawyer as his guardian," Dr. Merkin said. "The lawyer is filing the papers to have him admitted to the Beaumont State Center. An ambulance is coming tomorrow morning to transfer him. Just keep a watch on him and use those drugs if necessary."

"Will do Doc,"

"Well Dedra," he said, "they think I'm crazy, don't they? Well I've got news for them. As soon as we get outa here, were gonna bolt."